FINDING FISHER

M.J. James

A NineStar Press Publication

Published by NineStar Press
P.O. Box 91792,
Albuquerque, New Mexico, 87199 USA.
www.ninestarpress.com

Finding Fisher

Printed in the USA
First Edition
May, 2020

Print ISBN: 978-1-64890-011-2

Also available in eBook, ISBN: 978-1-64890-012-9

Warning: This book contains sexual content, which may only be suitable for mature readers, depictions of alcoholism, depression, drug/alcohol use, addiction, grief, hate crime, deceased family members, and suicidal ideation.

When Ian Fisher walked away from his life a year ago, he had no plans to ever return to where he grew up. However, after a run-in with the cops, he's forced to move in with his sister Rachel—in his dead parents' house.

Back home, Ian can't stop thinking about his ex, Sam. He still loves him and knows Sam loves him too, and he will stop at nothing to convince Sam to face his true feelings. But Sam has moved on. He has a fiancé, and he rejects Ian's repeated attempts to fix their relationship. Ian deals with those rejections by getting lost in the bottom of a bottle, refusing to face how messed up his life truly is.

After weeks in the hospital—the victim of a viscous hate crime—and learning of Sam's upcoming wedding, Ian has no choice but to fix his life to show Sam that he can be the man he needs. But rehab changes Ian, and he just might be ready to say goodbye to Sam forever.

Through addiction, violence, and self-preservation, Ian must learn to accept himself if he hopes to win back the man he loves.

As always, for Richard

Chapter One

Waking up in your own vomit sucked. For Ian Fisher, sleeping facedown in the previous night's dinner was more the norm than not. He had lost count months ago how many times he'd been jackknifed over a toilet as the sun came up, regurgitating the pain of the day before. Every single time, he remembered exactly how shitty his life had become and how bad he had fucked everything up. As last night's brew rumbled in his gut and he started to come around, things sure as hell smelled like any other day.

The rancid stench of stale beer that had stewed in stomach acid all night; the sour smell of piss-soaked pants, still warm against his crotch; the chalky taste of God knows how many different drugs clinging to the walls of his mouth. The all too familiar odors crept up his nose and down his throat, and Ian pulled himself off the floor. He stepped over people he didn't even know as he hugged the wall to the bathroom, ignoring the merry-go-round he could never get off. He had to piss. And puke. No time to choose so he did them both at once. Warmth snaking down his leg and the putrid stink slapping him in the face only made him heave harder into the toilet. Chunks of—shit, what had he eaten?—*something* plopped in the grungy bowl, the rot and funk watering his eyes. He shut off his brain like always, letting his body fend for itself until the torture ended. After emptying his gut, he slid to the floor and curled into the fetal position; the tiles cool against his skin.

What the fuck am I doing?

He had asked himself the same question before, hundreds of times over the past year or so. Each time, no answer. Just silence. This time, if he closed his eyes tight and blocked out the nausea and the pain and listened close, he could hear a faint voice, a whisper, repeating over and over in his head:

Stop, stop, stop.

He opened his eyes. The carnival ride that had become his life had begun its last revolution, the spinning slowing to a manageable speed. He gripped the bowl he'd just poured his guts into and pulled himself up. He rested against the rim, the chill of the porcelain blanketing his back in goose bumps. He wasted a quick second wondering where his shirt had disappeared to before shaking the thought from his head. No doubt the shirt was trashed, sopping wet with his own sick.

Though he took longer than last time, Ian somehow managed to stand. His newborn-like legs threatened to give him one last *fuck you* as they shook and wobbled. He braced against the vanity, eyes focused on a half-squeezed toothpaste tube, an old Tampax box, a couple of empty condom wrappers, anything to stop the urge to say "fuck this" and dunk his head in the toilet again. Once he had his center of gravity back on track, he raised his head.

Big mistake.

His reflection in the scum-streaked mirror hanging over the sink scared the hell out of him. He had aged well beyond his 24 years. Like something straight out of *The Walking Dead*. Like he had been rotting for, well, a year. Because he had. A slow, painful one. A deliberate one. A rot from the inside out. The decay had started deep, quiet and stealthy and hidden, but had begun to show around the edges, reaching the surface so others could see what he had known all along. He couldn't ignore this anymore. Time to choose: stop the rot, or let death consume him.

He slid achy hands over the faucet and gave the chrome fingers a slow turn before scooping up the cool water and drenching his face. Over. And over. And over. More water. Deluges of water. His eyes burned like a son of a bitch, but he kept up the onslaught. He scrubbed and scrubbed as he splashed, more desperate than ever to be clean. He needed a shower.

Nope. A shit idea if ever he had one. The room still spun like a top, and his legs were itching to give out on him. He kept drowning his face at the sink instead until his brain worked again. Well, as good as possible since he still floated in a cloud of crap left over by whatever the fuck he had ingested last night. A couple more handfuls of water before he picked up a towel and pressed the cotton against his face. He lingered over his eyes, scared to see his haggard reflection again. Every cell in his body wanted to turn around, walk out, and get drunk again. High again. Mind-numbingly wasted again.

No. Fuck that. Do it.

He dropped the towel and stared at himself. Stared hard at his reflection. The deep-set, blackened eye sockets. The sunken, pocked cheeks. Chapped lips. Greasy hair.

"Fuckin' loser," he eked out, his voice a jagged rasp, wedged between a whisper and early morning smoker's growl. He punched the mirror. Again. Again. Over and over until glass crawled deep under his skin and pushed blood from his veins.

He couldn't do this anymore.

Shit. He couldn't remember the last time he had thought those words. Not in the past year, for sure. He hadn't wanted to think dick in the past year. Just get drunk. Stay drunk. Get high. Stay high.

But now...

Ian shook his head. Crammed his hand in his pocket and pulled out salvation.

"Fuck it." One last glance at himself as the drug-of-the-moment skated over his mind and wiped out thoughts of fixing anything.

*

He woke up to the sound of bohemian music. A low melody thrumming in the background. The rhythm soothed him, kept him tripping on whatever he had fished out of his pocket. And 100 percent warped out of his mind was how he wanted to stay, numb and too fucked up to care or even think about anything. Ride the wave, let euphoria take him away from the shitty life he lived. The life he had created.

"Wanna go again?" Hands accompanied the deep, raspy voice vibrating in his ear. They massaged his pecs. Tickled his abs. Gripped his hard cock. He moaned and smiled, opened his eyes as a random guy went down on him. Ian grabbed a handful of black hair as the mouth worked magic on him, bringing him to the brink of orgasm. "Fuck, don't stop." Between the drugs and the blowjob, he experienced heaven. He started bucking his hips, ready to explode.

The mouth left his cock and traveled up his body, dipping into his abs and circling his nipples, sending him further over the edge than the drugs had already taken him, before crushing into his lips like a freight train. Ian shoved his tongue into the guy's mouth, tasting him. Cigarettes and whiskey, a flavor combination he had gotten used to over the past year, enveloped him. The odors were repulsive and magnetic at the same time, drawing him in deeper and deeper. He kissed with a fury he had never possessed before, like this would be his last. The guy kissed back with the same desperate want and need. They were in sync as much as two people high out of their minds could be, each knowing just what the other craved.

"Fuck me," the guy said, breathy and slurred when he pulled away from Ian's mouth. Ian stared into his eyes, deep pools of green so brilliant they were hypnotizing. Ian kissed him again, tugged on his plumped lips, and sucked his tongue into his mouth. The more the stranger moaned under his assault, the more Ian forged ahead.

He flipped the guy onto his stomach, trailing his back with his tongue. Gripped his muscular ass and buried his face there until the guy bucked beneath him, begging to be taken. And Ian did. He fucked him right there in the middle of whatever seedy motel he and his "friends" had the money for. Other people, Ian didn't know how many, littered the room but he didn't care. His could only focus on getting off. Something primal had taken over his senses, an animal instinct he couldn't control. He thrust into the stranger under him over and over as the guy moaned and cried out for more. Ian gave his all, getting lost in the drugged haze and sexual euphoria until he came and collapsed. Hands crawled up his chest and lips pressed against his as the drugs took over again, and he blacked out.

*

One second Ian rode the mother of all waves, fucking his brains out. The next he lay face down on puke-soaked carpet, hands twisted behind his back before being dragged out to the street like garbage. He could feel everything happening to him. Hear voices screaming out words his brain was too far gone to make out. Pain snuck into his high. Shattered the drug-induced reality. Left him alone in the dark.

He woke up who the hell knows how many hours later, his head throbbing so hard his stomach turned. He tried to move, sit up. Clearly the biggest mother fucker on the block had used him for target practice. He tried lifting his head instead. Nope, wasn't happening. He settled for opening his eyes. Well, *one* eye.

"What the fuck?" His throat ripped with every syllable like razor blades lined his esophagus. Jesus, he felt worse than death.

"Holy shit, man, we thought you were dead." Ian could hear the voice. Could half ass make out a shadow standing over him. "You okay, dude?"

He blinked over and over until the face came into focus. Long dark hair pulled into a tight pony. Tan skin muddled with scars from years of bad acne. Toothy grin. Ian thought he recognized the guy staring down at him. Andy? Archer? Who the fuck cared. Ian just wanted him to back the fuck up.

"Where are we?" he asked. Blood seeped into his mouth when he spoke. Shit.

"Jail, man. Fuckers got us, Fisher. They finally fucking *got us*." Andy/Archer/Whatever slumped to the floor next to Ian's head, and Ian couldn't tell if the sickening BO came from him or his own filth.

"Damn." He found the energy to sit up and leaned against the wall. Fucking merry-go-round ran top speed again.

"Yeah, man. Sucks big dick."

"I gotta get outta here." Ian closed his eyes and rubbed them. Kaleidoscopes of psychedelic colors and patterns spun in the darkness, and he had to stop before he puked all over the place.

"We all do, dude. None of us belong here."

"No, I mean out of this...*shit*." The word wasn't strong enough to encompass just how much Ian's life sucked. But it perfectly explained what he had left. Jack *shit*.

He had drunk and smoked and swallowed away everything. Apartment? Evicted. Job? Fired. Friends? Good ones were gone. Sam?

Fuck.

His head flooded with images and memories and feelings so fast his stomach flipped. Things he hadn't thought of or felt in two lifetimes took over his mind, his senses. Sam came rushing back in like a fucking freight train, ripping through the heart Ian had worked so hard to bury under too much drugs and alcohol.

Sam, Sam, Sam.

"No. No, no, no, no," Ian repeated, smacking his head against the wall behind him, hoping the pain of impact would crush the pain of remembering.

"Dude, you're gonna get locked up with the crazies, you keep this shit up." Andy/Archer/Whatever's voice barely registered.

"What?" Sam still lived there in his mind, his bright blue eyes Ian never wanted to stop seeing. The smile that always hit him hard right in the chest. *Mother fucking smile.* Sam's smile was Ian's Achilles' heel.

"They're gonna psych your ass for seventy-two, you keep on, man."

He thought about those words, what they meant. Hell, maybe getting three days of suicide watch would be a good thing. Free room and board. Good sleep. *Crazy* good drugs to help him not think of Sam.

Fuck no.

He had to get the hell out of there. Get drunk. Get high. Wash away Sam the old-fashioned way. But...God, he didn't want to. He didn't want to forget about Sam.

Did he?

Had someone asked him yesterday, he would've said, "Sam who?" Now, all he could think about was Sam's perfect fucking smile, and how he'd give a nut to see him again.

Yeah, he 100 percent had to get out of there.

Had to get to Sam.

"Hey!" Ian mustered enough strength to pull himself off the floor and stagger wobble-legged over to the bars keeping him and the world he hated so much apart. "Yo, guard!" A lanky man who had seen better days cut eyes at Ian from the waist-high counter he busily held up and raised a brow. Prick. "I want my phone call."

*

The room the guard dragged Ian to appeared twice as big as the holding cell he and about fifteen other guys were crammed into like stoned sardines, and if he tried, he bet he could reach out and touch two walls at the same time. A small table with a black box-style phone covered in buttons sat against the far wall, a round, backless rolling stool shoved underneath. The rest of the room sat sad and empty.

"Dial nine," Lanky Cop spouted. "You got three minutes." He stood in the doorway and stared at Ian. Ian wanted to walk over and knock his horse teeth down his fucking throat. He ignored the urge and shuffled over to the table. He used a foot to pull the stool from underneath and eased down onto the cushioned top. His head spun on the carousel; his body far past ready to throw in the fucking towel but... *Sam.* He's what kept Ian going, made him pick up the phone. He gave him the courage to call the one person he said he'd never ask for help from again the day he left town.

Well, the *second* person.

Three rings, then she answered. Ian swallowed. "Rach?" he said, trying his best to sound sober. "Rach, it's me. I fucked up."

Chapter Two

Ian tapped his fingers on the table in the empty room they stuck him in after lunch. He hadn't eaten the food they brought him, not like you could even call the shit on a plate food; pigs were fed better. His stomach stayed too wound up from the drugs and alcohol. Being in fucking jail didn't help either. His eyes danced around the room. Dull gray walls, bare and scuffed, paint chipping away in places. Years—decades—of filth packed into the corners of the floor. Half the ceiling tiles brown from leaks gone unnoticed.

How the hell did he end up there, so damn far from where he thought his life would take him? Sure, he'd had his share of beer and cheap liquor back in high school. He even took some X and oxy and all the other shit kids could buy on every corner in America. But he never thought he would end up sitting behind fucking bars. His life had become all so…overwhelming. There's a perfect damn word. He was *overwhelmed* by his life.

He yanked on the handcuffs chaining him to the table. Panic settled in. He needed to get up, walk around, bash his head on the fucking wall until darkness swallowed him up, took him away. His chest tightened as if being crushed by the ever-shrinking room trapping him. If he didn't get the fuck out—

The door buzzed, and he snapped back. He smiled when she stepped inside. He wanted to cry, but the

Andy/Archer guy had told him to stay strong, so he did. He couldn't help but be so damn glad to see her even though he never thought he would again.

"God, Ian, are you okay?" Rachel sat across from him and placed her hands on his.

"No touching," the guard who escorted her in said, his voice dry and stern, his eyes staring at the wall behind Ian. Rachel glared at him over her shoulder. He stood an average height, lanky, with hair too wispy and thin for someone so young. Ian figured he probably took this job so he could have power and control in his life or some other dumb bullshit. Rachel rolled her eyes but pulled her hands back.

"Jesus, Ian, what happened?" she asked.

Ian shook his head. "I don't know. I just—I messed up. Bad." He fought back tears as his sister stared at him, her own eyes welling up. God, even after a year of not seeing or speaking to her, the disappointment on her face still fucking killed him. To know he let her down over and over tore at him like a pack of rabid dogs. She was all he had, and he acted like he couldn't have cared less. "I'm so sorry," he added.

Rachel gave him a smile which carried up into her round green eyes. "It's okay. Don't cry."

Ian blinked. Tears streaked his face. "Fuck." He leaned forward and wiped his eyes with his shackled hands. "Been in here fuck knows how long and *now* I cry?" He smiled back, hoping to reassure her he was fine, which he wasn't. He hadn't been "fine" in a long fucking time. Didn't know if he ever would be again. "It's just, seeing you..." He stared at her, her sad eyes, and shook his head. "I shouldn't have called you. Not like this. This shouldn't have been the first time I called."

Rachel swiped at her own tears. "No," she agreed, "but I'm so glad you did. God, Ian, I've been so worried about you. I thought you..." She shook her head. More tears she had to brush away. "I'm just glad you called."

Ian glared at the ceiling. He took a deep breath and exhaled to get rid of the stress devouring him.

Stop crying stop crying stop crying.

He repeated the words over and over until he regained control of his crazy fucking emotions.

"So, what happens now?" Rachel asked. She wiped her runny nose on the sleeve of her shirt. Ian shook his head.

"Don't know," he said. "Public defender is supposed to be here around one."

"No way," Rachel protested. "We're getting you a real lawyer."

"Fuck no. I don't have 'real lawyer' money. And no way in hell you're paying a penny on me. And besides, the PD *is* a real lawyer."

"Yeah, who doesn't give a damn about you or anybody else he supposedly helps. All they care about is getting in and out as fast as they can." Ian smiled and sat back in the uncomfortable metal chair, and Rachel's brow rose. "What?" she asked. "Why are you smiling?"

"No reason," he said. "I'm just glad to see you." His sister had always been there for him. From bullies on the playground to fights with their parents when he became too much of a handful to bear, Rachel had been his unofficial bodyguard when they were growing up, always ready to bust a nose or black an eye to protect him. Nothing changed when he grew up.

Rachel smiled. "Ditto," she said, and Ian's nerves settled a bit. The panic choking him went away. His stomach stopped doing somersaults. He knew now, no matter what happened from then on, he would be okay, would survive because of her. "Okay," she went on, "so we're going with a public defender." She nodded like she had to convince herself. She glanced down at her watch. "I see being on time isn't his priority." Ian rolled his eyes as the door buzzed again, and a woman lugging a briefcase and a stack of papers rushed in.

"Oh my gosh, I'm so sorry I'm late. I'm normally on time for everything. Even early. But traffic was terrible. Are you Mr. Fisher? I'm Rita Sanchez. I'll be your public defender. Shall we get started? Wait, who's this?" She rambled so fast Ian only caught about half of what she spouted off in the five seconds since she walked in the room.

"Holy shit, lady. You okay?"

"What?" Rita asked, turning her attention toward him. She flashed a smile, but it disappeared faster than her words. "Oh, yes, fine, fine. You're Ian, right?"

"Uh, yeah, I'm Ian."

"I'm Rachel, his sister." Rita glanced and smiled, and Rachel's eyes were almost screaming *what the fuck?* at Ian across the table. "Are you *sure* you're okay?" she asked. "You seem...stressed."

Rita slid a chair from the corner and sat at the end of the table. Flipped through the stack of papers she'd carried in and pulled out one. "*I'm fine,*" she said again, a little more attitude in her voice than before; okay, *a lot* more attitude. Ian saw Rachel's neck turn red and her eyes squint. Oh yeah, she was about to—

"I'm sorry if our concern bothers you," Rachel snapped. "But when you charge in here like a linebacker and start spewing at the mouth you kind of freak me out a little. I mean, if there's somewhere else you need to be, please don't let my brother's *life* get in your way." Rachel crossed her arms over her chest and stared Rita down.

Rita stopped reading over the paper she'd plucked from the pile when Rachel spoke, sitting back in her chair and clasping her hands in her lap. After Rachel finished, she sat quiet. "Oh. Rachel, right?" Rita asked after realizing someone had just spoken to her. She leaned back up to the table. Rachel nodded after several seconds of quiet staring. "Well, Rachel, I apologize for bursting in so rudely. I never meant to make my client nor anyone else feel uneasy, or think I am not competent at my job. I assure you, I am *very* good at what I do. I love what I do. I pride myself on working hard and focusing on the best interests of my client. I am here for whatever either of you may need."

"Well, thank you," Rachel said. Ian winked at her when she turned to him, and she mouthed, "Shut up," and he had to bite his tongue not to laugh.

"You're very welcome," Rita said, picking up the paper again. "And there is *nowhere* else I need to be right now." Ian doubted Rita's smile was genuine. Rachel's either. "Now," she said, her eyes locking on Ian's, "let's focus on getting you out of here."

"Hell yeah," Ian said. "Best fucking thing I've heard all day."

*

Time sped and nearly reached four in the afternoon before they let Ian out. Rita worked her ass off, just like she had said she would, and Rachel posted his bond. Ian was pissed off more at himself than anything because, once again, his sister had to swoop in and save him. But he didn't argue when she insisted she didn't mind. He thanked them both the second they walked out of the jail together.

"No need to thank me," Rita said, fighting to keep hold of the loose papers in her arm as the three of them crossed the parking lot. "I'm just doing my job."

"Well, you're very good at what you do. So, thank you." Rachel surprised Ian and Rita both with her words. She had sat quiet almost the entire time back in the holding room when Rita detailed what Ian faced as far as the charges and possible punishment, only speaking if she didn't understand something. To hear her commend Rita on a job well done came out of nowhere.

"You're welcome, Rachel," Rita said with a smile Ian would bet she meant this time.

"So, what now?" Ian asked, opening the passenger door of Rachel's sedan.

Rita shifted the files in her arm. "Now, I go to bat for you. Try to get a lesser charge."

"You think you can?" Rachel asked. Rita eyed her. "I don't mean *can* you," she corrected. "Just—is there a chance they'll reduce his charges?"

"First-time offender, wrong place wrong time. I'm very confident I can get this dropped to a misdemeanor." Rita's eyes locked on Ian's. "As long as you stay out of trouble."

"No worries there," Rachel answered. "I'll chain him to the wall if I have to."

"There will be probation at the minimum," Rita went on, "so make sure he's ready for whatever happens."

Ian raised his hand. "Uh, *he* is standing right fucking here. And he's an adult and can take care of himself." Rachel and Rita both gave him the evil eye. "You know what I mean. I can stay out of trouble. And if I get probation, I'll make sure I don't fuck up again."

"Not *if*," Rita said. "Jail time is almost always followed with probation. But let's not worry about the possibilities right now." She pulled a set of keys from an open pocket on the side of her briefcase-bag thing and depressed the key fob. An alarm beeped, and the lights of the Lexus next to them blinked. "I'm heading to the district attorney's office now to file the appropriate paperwork; see if I can get in to see the prosecutor assigned your case." She opened the back door of her car and emptied her arms. "I have your number, Rachel." She opened the driver's door. "I will call the minute I know something. Shouldn't be more than an hour at most."

"Holy shit." Ian's stomach dropped. "An hour?" Before he knew if he'd be charged with drug trafficking. Fucking *drug trafficking*.

"Relax, Ian," Rita said, her voice calm for the first time since they'd met. "Like I said, I'm very good at my job." She gave them a smile, climbed in her car, and drove away.

Chapter Three

Rachel stayed quiet the first half of the drive home. Ian kept his mouth shut, scared to death to speak because he knew he didn't have the right say dick. He had been a fuck-up most of his life but never this bad. Never to the point he could maybe face some serious jail time. Even prison. He'd gone too far this time. Rachel wouldn't forgive him. How the hell could she?

Every few minutes he would steal a glance over, focus on her face, try to see if she secretly hated him and wouldn't express her true feelings until she thought no one would notice. He worried since he was out and safe, and she knew he hadn't ended up dead in a ditch somewhere, she would lay into him. Her wrath would happen sooner or later, he knew. He hoped for later. He'd had a shitty day. A shitty week. A shitty *year*. Rachel unleashing her fury about what a loser he had become would only make the day suck more. Even though he couldn't imagine feeling much worse than he already did. He had to call his sister to bail him out of fucking jail. They were going to charge him as a drug trafficker like some piece of garbage drug mule. And since he came to on a concrete bench in a damn jail cell, he couldn't stop thinking about Sam.

Fucking *Sam*.

Ian hadn't thought of Sam in months. Fought hard not to. Sam had always been the one thing he missed most about home. The *only* thing, really, besides Rachel. He didn't wanna go back. Had every plan to stay as far away from Chicago as he fucking could. The place held bad memories for him. His entire body hurt just thinking about the life he'd been living back then. After his parents died, he felt so empty, so fucking empty, being there. Like the city had nothing left for him.

Except Sam.

"Shit." He elbowed the window in frustration. He just wanted Sam out of his fucking head.

"Jesus, Ian!" Rachel reached out and smacked his arm. "You scared the crap out of me." She took a few deep breaths, and her hands gripped the steering wheel. "What is it?" she asked. "What's wrong?"

"Sorry," Ian said. "Nothing." He didn't want to have a conversation about Sam with her. Hell, he'd rather her go off on him about the fucking mess he had gotten himself in. Rachel loved Sam, loved Ian with Sam; if she thought for a second Ian wanted him back...

Did he? Want Sam? Want him back?

Fast as a flipped switch, Ian felt the heart-pounding, stomach-twisting feeling he hadn't had in forever. Not since he first met Sam. Since he fell in love with him. The memory swept over him, right there in the fucking car, like a wave. Drowning him in fucking *feelings*.

"Don't 'nothing' me." Rachel's voice made him jump. He had been so deep in the I-want-Sam pool. "You look like somebody kicked you in the shins."

"More like the nuts," Ian said, staring out the window.

"Okay." Rachel shifted in her seat and tightened her grip on the wheel. "Wanna talk about it?"

"Nope." Last fucking thing he wanted. Ever. He didn't wanna talk about Sam or think about Sam or fucking *miss* Sam. Jesus.

"Fine," Rachel said. "Food then." She yanked the wheel, and the car shot to the right, flying up the exit ramp just inches from the guardrail.

"Shit!" Ian dug his fingers so deep into the dashboard, he knew there'd be indentions.

"Calm down," Rachel said, taking a left at the top of the exit. She floored the gas and slid in front of a Chevy Tahoe, who blew their horn. "When did you get so dramatic?"

"Uh, about the time you became a fucking psycho behind the wheel." He took a few deep breaths and pried his fingers from the dashboard. "Why are you in such a damn hurry?"

"I'm not. I'm just hungry. Ooh, look, a Denny's. Your favorite."

Ian laughed. "You're a terrible liar, Rach. Seriously. Awful." She smiled and ignored him. "And I haven't eaten at fucking Denny's since I was a kid."

"Doesn't mean it's not your favorite."

Ian shook his head but couldn't hide his smile when they pulled in and parked.

He did love Denny's.

*

Ian sucked down two cups of coffee like water once they sat down at a booth in the corner. He'd still had cottonmouth from last night, and there wasn't a chance in hell he would drink a drop of anything while in lock-up. God only knew what kind of rancid shit they'd serve in jail. Hell, he'd bet even the water would kill you.

He eyed Rachel as he sipped on a third cup of straight black coffee. She seemed impatient. Sure, she tried hard *not* to, tried even harder to appear right as rain sitting in a random restaurant on a random exit off the interstate on her way home with her loser brother she'd just bailed out of jail, but Ian knew better. He may have disappeared for the last year, ignoring the shattered pieces left of his family by killing himself with drugs and whiskey and sex with strangers, but one thing he hadn't been able to drown out was how well he knew his sister. He'd been born with the ability to see right through the walls she would put up. Her fake smiles. Her attempts to keep the peace when he knew she really wanted to lash out. And right now, he knew without a doubt she itched to tear into him. After the waitress refilled his cup and left, she couldn't hold back any longer.

"Talk," she said, sipping her own steaming cup of coffee and glaring at him from across the table. Ian took his time with his third cup, adding in creamer and a couple packets of fake sugar from the pink wrappers crammed into the little glass bowl on the table. "If you think I won't leave you here, think again, little brother."

"God, please do." He stirred the coffee and took a sip, the warmth a nice contrast to how cold he felt. The temperature had dropped to about forty degrees outside—and at least another ten degrees colder in jail.

Rachel flung a pink sweetener packet at him. "*Talk,*" she repeated.

"And say what?" Ian asked. He drummed his fingers on the Formica tabletop. Could've been the coffee he'd guzzled on an empty stomach, but he would bet he stalled because he had no fucking desire to get into the unavoidable argument-slash-overbearing lecture with her in the middle of a restaurant.

"Don't play dumb with me. What have you been doing all these months? Where did you go? Why didn't you come home, or at least call me, so I'd know you were alive?"

"Jesus." Ian moved to get up.

"Sit down, Ian."

"You're not my mother."

"I don't care. *Sit.*" Ian locked eyes with her, unmoving for several uncomfortable seconds before giving up and slinking back into his seat like a scolded puppy. "You've been running for over a year. You've run far enough."

Ian laughed. "Not even fucking close."

"No? Oh, okay. Then tell me... Where do you think you can go where your problems can't find you, huh? The bottom of a bottle of booze? Or pills?"

"Booze?" Ian said with a laugh. His skin crawled, and he wanted the conversation to stop. "What are you, a hundred?"

"Stop making jokes and answer me."

He shrugged, frustrated. "I don't know, Rach. Maybe."

"Oh yeah? And how has drinking yourself to death been working out for you so far? Your life all good now? Problem free?"

"Fuck you. What's your deal? Trying to make me feel shittier than I already do?" Ian slumped back in his seat and folded his arms across his chest. "Stop wasting your fucking time."

"I'm just trying to get you to *wake up*, Ian. To see how running away doesn't solve anything."

"I didn't run away."

"What would you call disappearing in the middle of the night?"

"I didn't disappear. I left a note."

Rachel laughed. "You're kidding, right? 'See ya, sis' is not a note you leave when you're gonna take a year to run off and screw up your life. Look at me. *Look. At. Me.*" Ian huffed but lifted his head and stared at her. "I love you, okay? It's the only reason I'm so hard on you. Before and now. Because I love you. I want you to...*grow up* already. You're twenty-five years old. Past time to get your life together."

"What do you care?"

"Really? You're gonna ask me of all people why I care?" Ian widened his eyes and nodded. A childish, dick move he knew, but he had gotten too pissed to give a damn. Rachel sat back and went stone quiet. Didn't speak, didn't move. Just sat there. Ian wanted to apologize—knew he should have—but kept quiet too. Rachel's entire demeanor all of a sudden changed. She went from pretty pissed off to almost sad in less than two seconds.

"I searched for you," she said, so low Ian almost didn't hear her. He had no clue how to respond. Between the look on her face and how fucking depressed she sounded, he thought she might be about to flip out on him. "Not enough, apparently, but I did. I called hospitals, shelters. Hell, I even checked morgues. I couldn't find you."

"Rach, I—"

"For almost nine months," she went on, ignoring him. Ian wanted her to stop because her words hurt his chest, but he let her keep talking. "I finally had to stop though. Spending day after day after day trying to find you just got to be too much." She stopped talking and stared past him. She was probably reliving how she must've felt to think her own brother lay in a fucking morgue somewhere. Ian's stomach turned.

"Don't do this," he said, his voice weak.

"What? Don't tell you how it killed me to think of you out there all alone, scared, maybe hurt? Or God forbid, worse?" She blinked rapidly; Ian had already lost the battle against his tears. He kept his head down. Wiped the pain streaking his face in secret. His heart scorched his chest, frantic to be let out.

"Trying to find somebody who doesn't want to be found consumes you, Ian. Constantly searching and making phones calls and being scared to death when an unidentified body shows up somewhere just...takes over *everything* in your life. I couldn't sleep. Barely ate. Chris left, not that our separating had anything to do with you. Our marriage ended way before you vanished. But I didn't even notice because I had been so focused on finding you. Making sure you were okay. Spending every minute of my life focused on finding you nearly killed me. I didn't want to stop, but I knew I had to. And all you can say is fuck you, what do you care?" Ian's head shot up and he stared at her. "Yeah, I know the *F* word, too, Ian." She sat back and watched him.

"What do you want me to say?" he asked, his tears giving way to anger. He didn't want to be pissed at her. Didn't want to take out his disgust with himself on her. He was just so mad he didn't think he could stop.

Rachel threw her hands up and smirked. "Oh, I don't know. How about, 'thanks, sis, for caring so much?' Or, 'I appreciate you dropping everything to drive hours to bail my ungrateful ass out of jail.'"

"Don't worry, I'll find a way to get you your money back."

"Jesus. I'm not—stop acting like a brat, Ian. I don't give a shit about the money. Or the time. I care about *you.*"

"Fuck. If this is you caring, I'll take a hard pass."

"Why did you call me, then? I mean, if you wanted somebody who would drive up here, pay your bail, and then drive you back home without saying a word about the fact you're killing yourself, then why me? You should know me well enough to know this is how I would be."

Ian sat quiet. Rachel eyeballed him. He sat up. Stared at her. Spoke without thinking, his brain too fried, his heart too damaged to stop. "Because I thought..." He fiddled with a sugar packet on the table in front of him, trying so hard to shut up. He just wanted to shut off his fucking emotions, go numb, forget. He twirled the little pink packet back and forth through his fingers, buying time he didn't have. "I thought you might still care enough about me to help me." His tears were back. This time he didn't hide them. He kept his head up so she could see him, see the *real* him. Broken. Afraid. Desperate. Before he knew what was happening, she stood next to him. Pulling him close to her. Holding him tight. Laying his head against her chest while he cried right there in his favorite childhood restaurant.

Chapter Four

The crazy-ass dinner they'd just had drained Ian's resolve. Laughing, fighting, crying, crying, crying. By the time they were hitting the interstate again, he had passed out. He dreamed of Sam and Rachel and his parents. All the people he loved most. They were all there, still in his life. And he felt happy. Happy because he hadn't run away. Hadn't gotten arrested. Hadn't fucked up his life so bad he couldn't be saved. In the dream life, he and Sam were together. Rachel was still married and in love. His parents were alive, laughing and living life to the fullest. The dream had been the best he'd ever had, and he wanted to stay buried deep inside his own mind until reality caught up.

"You need a shower. Like, *yesterday.*" The sound of Rachel's voice jolted him awake. He groaned, wishing he could go back to sleep where life had been better. He rubbed his eyes and yawned. He had slept all the way to her house.

"Oh, like you smell like peaches." He yawned again and watched raindrops roll down the windshield of the car.

"At least I don't smell like a sewer. I could scrub for a week and never get your stink out of my seat." He gave her the finger, his go-to "fuck off." Rachel laughed. "Come on," she said. "Get inside and hop in the shower, and I'll throw your clothes in the wash." The weight of his life sat on top of him, making him tired as hell, and he just wanted sleep. But did as ordered. He made a beeline for the bathroom, stripping his grimy shirt off in the hall. As if somebody had flipped a damn switch, he couldn't wait to get clean and wash the puke, piss, and jail off.

The water practically scalded his skin, and he relished in the heat. He closed his eyes, let the water pour over him, wash away the filth. Or at least try. Thoughts of Sam filled his head. Ian wondered what Sam's life had been like the past year. He hoped he'd had a good one and not wasted time on missing him. Or hating him. Like how Ian's life had been right after he left town. He could think of nothing but Sam twenty-four-seven back then. His heart had been obliterated, destroyed. It would've taken a lifetime to repair, so he had just finished the job with drugs and whiskey instead. But Sam... Sam always found a way in. He had always been there, tucked away in the smallest part of Ian's heart that still held strong to the knowledge Ian would seek him out one day. And apparently the day had come. He jumped from the shower, ran a towel over his body to soak up the bulk of the water before wrapping the flowery fabric around his waist and heading out. He found Rachel coming from the laundry room just off the kitchen.

"No clothes," he said, gesturing to his naked torso. For the first time since, shit, he couldn't remember, he started feeling like his old self. Could've been being back in Chicago where he grew up, in the house where he grew up, but he knew his renewed purpose had to be because of Sam. The man he fell in love with, never fell *out* of love with, lived only a couple of neighborhoods away. Knowing Sam was so damned close invigorated Ian like nothing else ever had. His pain hadn't left, though. It still sat under his skin like a disease waiting to cripple him and pull him under, but he was ready to fight now. Ready to fight to get Sam back. Get his life back.

"God, that was fast," Rachel said, pulling the laundry room door closed. "I just got the wash going. I'll get you some of Chris's." She smiled and headed to her bedroom.

"So, the prick still has shit here?" Ian asked, following her.

"The *prick* is my husband. Kind of." She pulled a large plastic bin from the bottom of her walk-in closet—the closet his parents had shared his entire life—and began rummaging through the contents.

"*Was* your prick husband. Now just a prick, like I said."

Rachel stopped for a second. "Wow. You actually *were* listening." He flipped her off again, and she smiled and kept digging. She fished around for another minute before pulling out a pair of jeans and white button-down from the bottom of the bin. "Here." She tossed them to him. "All I have left of his."

"Thanks." He stared at the clothes in his hands. "Guess I need to go home sometime," he said. "Grab some of my own clothes and stuff."

"What all do you have?"

He cut his eyes at her. "I have shit, Rach. I'm not homeless. I'm just..."

"Just what?" She folded her arms over her chest.

Ian opened his mouth. Closed his mouth. Shook his head. "Fuck."

"Oh, I almost forgot," Rachel called out. Ian stopped at the door and turned around. "Rita called while you were in the shower. She got your possession charged dropped to a misdemeanor accessory something or other."

Ian cocked a brow. "Which means?"

"Which means you get probation. No jail time."

He felt a bit of weight lift off him. "Damn. She *is* good."

Rachel nodded and smiled. "Very good," she agreed. "You only got ninety days."

"Holy shit, for real?"

"Yep."

"Wow. Awesome. I mean, I can't believe it."

"There's a catch though."

Ian's stomach dropped. "Of course, there is."

Rachel shoved the bin back in the closet underneath the hanging clothes and closed the door. She wiped nonexistent dust from her hands as she said, "You have to stay here."

He shrugged. "No big deal, I guess. I mean, I didn't wanna come back here, but I like Chicago."

Rachel shook her head. "No," she said. "Not Chicago. *Here*. As in, live in this house."

Ian took a deep breath. Glanced around her bedroom for a second. He wanted to say, "fuck no, no way" and turn and run back to the life he had let consume him the past year, the life he had let destroy him from the inside out because running away would be so much easier than trying to fix things. To fix the thousands of mistakes he'd made. Instead he said, "You know what's crazy?"

"What?" Rachel asked.

"I thought I'd never see this place again. For real, I thought I'd never come back to this house. Stand in this room. Smell the smells and see the memories. Now I'm court-ordered to live here for the next three months." He made eye contact with Rachel and nodded. "I left and never wanted to come back. But not because of you, Rach.

I promise. I didn't wanna come back to this house, you know?" So many emotions stirred deep inside him and he struggled to keep them in check. He wanted to cry. Wanted to run away again. Wanted to punch enough holes in the walls of *their* house the entire thing would collapse and bury him right along with all the painful memories.

Rachel's voice was soft when she spoke. "What about after? After probation?" she asked. Her words pulled him back to reality. He stared at her, kneeling in front of his mom's old laundry basket sitting on the floor full of clothes *not* his mom's. His heart broke a little more.

He sighed and glanced at the ceiling. "After?" he repeated. "I'll let ya know." He met her gaze again, and she nodded.

"Fair enough." He nodded back and stepped out long enough to drop his towel and throw the clothes on. Tried to ignore the urge to break down right there in the hall as he tugged the jeans up his legs and buttoned them. He felt funny going commando. He hadn't walked around without underwear since high school but didn't have time to dwell. He went back to Rachel's room—*not Mom's*—as she placed the last of the clothes she'd been folding into the dresser drawers. She jumped when she saw him.

"Geez, Ian, you scared the crap out of me. I thought you'd left."

"Sorry," he said. "But I, uh, I am. Leaving, I mean." Her eyes grew wide.

"What? You just said—"

"Not *leaving* leaving," he interrupted. "I mean I'm going out. Tonight. Don't look at me all judgmental. It's not what you think." He ran a hand through his hair, frustrated. Antsy. "I just—I gotta go see him."

She eyed him for a second before she realized who he meant. "Oh. Sam."

"Yeah." He lowered his eyes. Twisted his fingers. Looked back up at her. "Don't worry, okay? I'll be fine."

"Ian—"

"Rachel, chill out. I said I'm fine. I just *have* to see him. Talk to him." He stopped talking, his voice caught in his throat, strangled by the pain and fear living there. "I...still love him."

Rachel nodded. "I know, sweetie. But please don't—" She paused a second. "—please be careful."

Ian smiled. "I will. Promise." He left the room again, but something compelled him back. "Hey?" he called out, worried he'd scare her again she seemed so on edge.

"Yeah?" She busied herself with refolding some T-shirts she'd pulled out of a drawer but stopped when he walked in.

"I just wanted to say, uh—" His words caught in his throat again, so he walked over and wrapped his arms around her instead.

She laughed and did the same to him. "What's this for?"

Ian held her tight. Closed his eyes and let his hug linger. "I love you," he whispered, so low even he almost couldn't hear himself. He slipped from her arms and walked away, holding back tears as he left the room.

Chapter Five

Ian planned to go see Sam, just like he'd said. But coming face to face with the guy he walked out on, the only person who had been there for him—not to mention the last twenty-four hours of hell he'd gone through—he needed alcohol first. Lots of alcohol. Yeah, he knew he couldn't drink on probation. But when had doing the right thing ever been his first choice?

He also knew how drinking had been his coping mechanism, his crutch, somewhere deep down. The fact didn't make him give a shit one way or the other though, knowing he used alcohol to deal with life. Ignoring everything important had been his plan, if you could call drinking your problems into oblivion a plan, since the night he had decided to say fuck everything and bail. He got drunk first. The feeling of freedom being shitfaced gave, like all his cares and fears and worries were gone, had invigorated him, made him feel alive again for the first time since his parents had died. He never wanted the feeling to end. And up until his arrest, he got just what he wanted. But now, about to go a year back in time by seeing Sam again, those cares and fears and worries were springing up like weeds after a rainstorm and he had to tamp them back down.

He was glad the walk from Rachel's to the only bar in town worth a shit had been a fast one. He didn't want to have time to talk himself out of doing what he had no doubt would be in the top five biggest fuck ups of his life. He had never been a make-a-list type of guy, but you couldn't help remember the times you screwed shit up for yourself in a major way, sear them into your memory forever. Getting kicked out of college, losing his job, losing *Sam*, they were all fighting for top billing. But *chasing* Sam... What the hell was he thinking?

He wasn't. Which is why his life had fallen apart. Why he'd had to call Rachel to bail him out. Why he agreed to the crazy idea of moving back to the hellhole town he swore he'd never step foot in again instead of begging his public defender to get the judge to let him live somewhere, *anywhere*, else. He hadn't been thinking right since he stepped foot back in Chicago. Because of Sam. Because missing Sam had started eating him from the inside out since he woke up in jail and only got worse when he knew they were in the same city. His need to see Sam consumed him, took over his ability to be rational, to the point he couldn't think of *not* seeing him. All the time and energy he'd wasted trying to get over not having Sam in his life anymore, the effort he'd put into forgetting about Sam altogether, vanished in a split second the minute he thought of him again. He had been so stupid and childish running away, only to come back anyway.

"Fuck off," he said aloud to the voices in his head and went inside the bar.

Jack shit had changed. As far as Final Draft was concerned, the past year hadn't even happened. He hated the name of the place. The original owner had been a wannabe writer or some shit and thought a stupid pun would give everybody a laugh. Ian got the play on words, yeah, but understanding the why didn't mean the name wasn't dumb as hell. But as long as his glass stayed full, they could call the place whatever the fuck they wanted.

Like the corny ass name, everything else about Final Draft was a picture straight out of his memory. Same ugly ass blood-red paint and brown laminate tables. Same drunks scattered around like leeches after a rainstorm. Same grungy lighting so bad you couldn't see your hand in front of your face sometimes. Darkness drenched the place at barely past noon. Half-sized windows butted up to the ceiling, forever stained yellow and brown by years of nicotine, did shit for letting in any natural light. The floors were coated in a foot of grime, dirt, spit, and vomit from alcohol newbies who couldn't hold their liquor, and the air reeked of old cigarettes and even older men. The bar was a living, breathing time machine most people would have turned their nose up at and ran like little bitches. But Ian fucking *loved* every single thing about it. He loved the familiarity. Just like home. Where he belonged. Where he fit. And on the night he planned to see Sam again for the first time in a lifetime, his sitting at the bar couldn't have been more perfect because Final Draft was where they had first met.

They were both twenty-one. Ian had been for a few months, Sam a newbie. The night he came in had been Sam's birthday, in fact, and some of his friends had dragged him to the bar as a rite of passage. By the time Ian got there, Sam had already been lit like a fucking Christmas tree, laughing and having a good time, tossing back tequila shots like water. Ian had been attracted to him the second he saw him. Sam was beautiful, which had been obvious to anyone with eyes, but his physical appearance wasn't the only thing irresistible about him. He always seemed so comfortable and free, two things Ian had never been a single day in his life. He had been too scared to go over and talk to Sam, say hi, so he'd sat at the bar and watched him. Almost an hour had gone by before Sam caught Ian staring. Freaked the fuck out, Ian blushed and turned away. Sam had been the one who sauntered over, the one who started the conversation Ian had wished he'd been ballsy enough to do. They had hit things off from the get-go and were together from then on. Until Ian ran.

Mad and hurt and so fucking full of regret, Ian forced the memory out of his head before he ended up crying in the damn bar. Fuck, he was like a walking chick flick. He took a seat and gave the lacquered oak slab a knock.

"Who's a guy gotta blow to get a beer in this shithole?" he called out with a smile. Just being there, surrounded by the smells and the dank air and other lovers of the drink, made him happy. Or at least he *felt* happy. Which he hadn't been since—*No*. No Sam. Not yet. Thinking of Sam before he had time to take the edge off would fuck everything up.

"Son of a bitch. Check out what last night's leftovers dragged in." A short redhead only inches taller than the bar she busily wiped down looked like somebody had just kicked her in the teeth. "Ian. Fucking. Fisher. What the hell are you doing here?"

"Nice way to treat your patrons, Stacey. No wonder this place has gone to shit."

Stacey laughed. "Fuck you, Fisher." She filled a glass from the tap and slid the liquid courage down to him. "Seriously, though, what brings you back? Good to see ya, but I thought you hated this town?"

"Oh, I do," Ian said, downing half the beer in one gulp. Fuck, it felt good. Like a best friend come home. "Got in a little trouble, is all. Figured I'd get myself *out* of trouble here."

Stacey smirked. "You? Trouble? Get the fuck outta here."

"Fuck you, Red."

"Been there already, remember? Or has chasing dick fried your brain?"

Ian shrugged. "Wanted to try. See what the fuss was about. And you were giving the shit away back then, so—"

"You asshole!" Stacey threw her dirty towel at him and he laughed.

"And the dick chases *me*, just so ya know."

"Yeah, I bet dick chases you." She slid another pint his way. "So," she asked, snagging the towel she'd flung at him and giving the draft station a rubdown. "Everything okay with you? For real?" Ian chugged the second beer faster than the first and signaled for another. Stacey filled two glasses and brought them over.

"You seen Sam?" he asked, taking a huge swallow from the fresh pilsner. He would need a lot more for what he planned to go do.

"Easy, Fisher," she said, wiping up a bit he spilled. She watched as he ignored her and took another gulp. "Haven't lately," she finally answered. "But I'm here all the damn time so I doubt I would have anyway."

Ian nodded. "Yeah, he never liked slumming with us down here very much, huh?" He finished off the third beer and wrapped his hand around the fourth she had ready for him. God, he loved this woman.

"Not with all of us."

Ian caught her smile. "Funny."

Stacey cleared away all the empty mugs and dropped them into a plastic bin beneath the bar. "So, is he why you came back?" she asked. "Because of Sam?"

Ian finished off the beer and stood up. His head swam and swirled and he had to blink a few times to focus. Perfect.

"Told ya," he slurred through the haze in his mind. "Trouble."

Stacey laughed as he stumbled out of the bar. "Yep. You sure as shit are."

Chapter Six

Ian could find Sam's house in his sleep. He had been around so much when they were together most people in the neighborhood thought he lived there anyway. He wanted to. Sure as shit would have if Sam had just asked, but...

Nope. Not dwelling on the past. New night, new start. He would get Sam back. Since he woke up in jail, he could think of shit else. Just Sam. He had tried not to, but his heart won out, made him remember. Now, memories of Sam consumed him. Which fueled his need to go see him the first chance he got.

He fumbled his way down Sam's street, clinging to the waist-high fences lining the sidewalks for balance. Christ, four beers had almost done him in. Which made zero fucking sense because he had become somewhat of a pro at holding his liquor. He figured there must've been some leftover effects of whatever he had taken the other night, because he wasn't a fucking lightweight. He prided himself on his partying skills.

The neighborhood reminded him of a fucking magazine photo. All the houses were practically the same, with their earthy colors like brown and green and the weird orange-but-not-orange a lot of flowerpots were made of. And speaking of flowers, both sides of the entire street were covered in them. They were planted around the trees, hiding the bottoms of all those fences he used as a cane; hell, people even shoved them into old wheelbarrows and fucking bathtubs and sat them on their front lawns like some crazy ass version of art. He loved the place once. Now, bumbling his way down the street, he was overwhelmed how fucking perfect everything seemed.

Just like Sam.

Ian knew good and well Sam wasn't *actually* perfect. At least not by the definition of the word. But to him, Sam couldn't have been better. His kindness was off the charts. Like, cross the street to lend a hand off the charts. He had a heart bigger than anybody Ian had ever known. He would go out of his way to help people, which always kind of freaked Ian out because he didn't care to meet a stranger at all, but he sure loved how much Sam did. And in their relationship, Ian knew Sam outshined him in every way. Where Ian lacked, Sam carried them. He did everything he fucking could to hang onto Ian, and Ian thanked him by bailing on him like a pussy. Those were some reasons why, in Ian's eyes, Sam could be nothing but perfect. And the reasons why Ian wanted him back.

He found Sam's house drunk and in the dark, smiling when he did because he knew he could, and stood at the end of the walk. Like the bar, the house hadn't changed a bit. Of course, the entire town stayed stuck in the fucking past so Sam's place staying the same was no surprise. Ian could just make out the color. A bright sky blue, the same as Sam's eyes. Fuck, those eyes. Made him hard just picturing them. So soulful. Kind. A blue you could get lost in, and be just fucking fine staying lost forever. And Ian had. Every day they were together, he had. And he loved being lost there. Loved those eyes. Loved Sam. Jesus, why the fuck had he left?

"Fuckin' moron is why," he said out loud. "Didn't know what your dumbass had." He stood there shaking his head a minute, dragging his foot in the dirt. The night bordered on too cold to function, nearing thirty degrees already, but Ian didn't care. He felt way too wound up to care. He couldn't stop thinking about what his life would have been like had he stayed with Sam. Just. Fucking. *Stayed.* They would no doubt be living together by now. Maybe even married. Either way they would be together, happy, living life instead of *avoiding* living life like Ian had done for so long now he couldn't even remember how. But everything was so much easier when you avoided anything real. No worries, no problems. Just numb.

Ian laughed and shook his head, the beer he'd pounded like a frat pledge back at Final Draft hitting him like a semi full of cinderblocks. He had gotten so used to being in a constant state of just-before-drunk pretty much every day since leaving town he had almost forgotten what a real buzz felt like. The kind of buzz experienced by normal, *sober* people when they drank, not a loser who treated alcohol like water or breath mints. He shrugged off whatever the hell had tried to slither in and started up the walk. Tripped over a buckled piece of concrete. Nearly broke his fucking toe kicking the shit out of the bulging slab and almost went down.

"Fuck!" He righted himself and headed up onto the porch. He waited a few seconds. To make sure he was doing the right thing or to get the courage, he didn't know. Just waited. His heart thrummed in his chest, his head, his ears. He ignored the sound. Lifted his hand and rang the bell.

What are you fucking doing, Ian?

Damn. Same question twice in as many days. He felt like a possessed preppy college fucker who spent all his time talking about his feelings and shit. Ian couldn't have been more opposite of a frat boy. He fought too damned hard to let out what had been eating him alive inside. He sure as hell didn't want people knowing just how miserable he felt, how much he hated himself all the damn time. Fuck. That.

Ian eyed the door. The knob didn't budge. Not a fucking inch. He stared and stared and the damn knob *wasn't fucking moving*. He ran a hand over his face and stepped back.

Shit.

Doubt crept in. Made him rethink what the hell he was doing. Why in the hell did he think Sam would even talk to him, let alone take him back? He was a fucking loser who couldn't get his shit together if his life depended on it. What did he have to offer Sam now? Before, he had been in a good place in his life. Now...

He shook his head trying to force out the doubt and rang the bell again. He knocked on the door when no one answered and turned to leave just as the lock clicked. He heard the scrubbing sound of a door being slowly opened. His heart rate spiked. Heat flooded his face, down his chest and abs. His entire body twitched with anticipation. A year. A fucking year since—Sam's face appeared in front of him before he had time to process.

God, Sam's face. Just as perfect and sexy and inviting as the first time Ian had laid eyes on him. And the last. Ian had fucking missed his face. Missed seeing, touching, *loving* his face. And now more than ever he wanted Sam's face back. Wanted Sam back. Fucking *needed* Sam back.

"Jesus. *Ian*?" Sam stepped out onto the porch. "Oh my God."

Ian smiled as he looked Sam over. He hadn't changed at all. He still had the same awkward shyness about him, like he wasn't good enough to be wanted or loved. Sam's genuine obliviousness to how amazing he was made Ian crazy hot. His dick pulsed.

"Hey, Sam," he said, not blinking in case a dream had taken over his mind. "God, you look amazing." Sam wore a pair of baggy pajama pants and an old T-shirt, glasses instead of contacts, and sported some major bedhead. But Ian only saw those eyes. Eyes he desperately wanted to stare into for the rest of his damn life. Then seeing Sam's body seized his brain. The body he had worshiped more times than he could count. And the sexiness oozing off Sam with ease.

"Ian, I—Jesus, I don't even know what to say. What are you doing here?" Sam seemed shocked, even to drunk Ian. He pulled the door closed behind him and folded his arms over his chest to try to stay warm. Ian wanted to wrap his arms around him so the cold couldn't touch him.

"Came to see you," he said instead. He reached out and palmed Sam's stomach, hard abs pushing against his hand beneath the thin material. Ian's entire body came alive at the touch. "Fuck, I've missed you."

Sam stepped back until his hand slipped away. "My God. I just can't believe you came back here."

Ian stopped smiling and stared into Sam's eyes. Still crazy good blue, but...different somehow. "Can I get a hug?" He ignored what Sam had said and moved in, arms open.

"No, Ian. I—" He didn't get to finish rejecting Ian because Ian crashed into him, knocking them both into the door.

"Jesus!" Sam held them both up and Ian felt like fucking heaven because they were pressed so close together and he could smell Sam and touch him and feel him trembling against him and now life couldn't be more fucking *perfect*. "You're drunk."

"Maybe a little," Ian said, his speech so slurred he'd be surprised if Sam understood him. He had to fight the urge to lick the exposed skin of Sam's neck, which sat right in fucking front of him, as he inhaled the natural musk of Sam's existence. His brain flashed memory after memory like a slideshow as the scent washed over him. His dick turned to granite in his pants.

"Ian! Move." Sam pushed Ian upright and glared at him.

Ian flashed an I-want-you smile. "God, I've missed you." He brought a hand to Sam's neck. Held his fingers there, Sam's pulse vibrating his skin. The heat coming from him was like rocket fuel. Ian could have fucked him right there on the porch and shocked the hell out of Sam's Norman Rockwell neighborhood.

"Don't. Please." Sam put his own hand over Ian's, trying to pry his fingers from his neck. Ian ignored him and intertwined their fingers instead. He used to love holding hands with Sam. He would grip Sam's hand every chance he got. The simple gesture of having his hand locked with Sam's had always calmed him. And tonight felt no different.

"You miss me?" Ian asked. He kept his smile, but his eyes were heavy as fuck and his knees wanted to stop holding his drunk ass up. He swayed and stumbled, and Sam moved to catch him. Hold him up. Like before. Like always.

"God, you are so wasted." He slid an arm around Ian's waist and Ian felt every fucking inch of Sam's skin against him. His skin pulsed with electricity, so familiar. Right. Like pure fucking heaven as Sam held him tight against him and opened the door. Warmth slapped him—from the house, from Sam—and he welcomed the heat. He slid an arm around Sam's shoulders to keep from falling. His hand wandered, fingers tracing the muscle beneath them.

Before he even realized, they were in Sam's house. He was sitting on Sam's couch. Sam stood at the end. He took off Ian's shoes. Pulled a blanket up to his chest. Ian wanted to reach out to him, pull him onto the couch with him so he could hold him again, kiss him. But his arms wouldn't work. His legs gave up. His eyes were so fucking heavy he couldn't stop them from closing, blocking out the beauty standing over him.

"I love you, Sam," he managed to say before darkness took over and he was gone.

Chapter Seven

Ian's head hurt like a son of a bitch. Nothing new, big surprise, but... Four beers? *Four beers?* Felt like a fucking case, going by the headache. His skull throbbed and pounded and did jack shit for his spinning gut. The sunlight pouring in through the floor-to-ceiling window on the wall behind the couch didn't help either. Damn Rachel and her up-with-the-roosters mornings.

Wait...

Fuck, he wasn't *at* Rachel's. Or his own apartment. Or even some random guy's motel room. He had slept at Sam's.

Shit.

The realization woke him up like a fucking bucket of ice water to the face. He shot up off the couch—and fell right back onto the plush fabric.

"Fuck." If he didn't know Stacey better, he would've sworn she roofied him last night. Thick fog covered his face. Suffocated him. His head spun like a top and he had to keep swallowing back vomit. And sometime during the night he must've eaten a bucket of fucking cotton.

He stood up slower this time. Took a few seconds to gain his balance before heading to the kitchen for some water. Or a fucking bullet, whichever he found first.

"Woah, shit!" Ian almost lost it, his balance *and* the beer in his gut. There was a guy in Sam's kitchen. A half-naked guy. Hot. Tall. Smiling.

In. Sam's. Kitchen.

"Sorry," the guy said. "Didn't mean to wake you up. Sam said you were a light sleeper."

What the fuck?

The guy just kept smiling as he filled a mug with coffee and scrambled some eggs on the stovetop, and the entire scene weirded Ian the fuck out.

"Uh..." What should he say? "Hey."

"Noah," the guy said. "I'd shake your hand, but..." He gestured to the eggs and a pan of French toast on the island stovetop in front of him. Like this shit couldn't be more normal, him being there, cooking breakfast. The words *get the fuck out of our house, dick* filled Ian's head.

Ian took a step back. "It's cool. Cool." Not cool. Not by a fucking long shot.

"Oh. Hey, guys." Sam snuck up on them and Ian almost jumped. This whole shirtless-guy-cooking-eggs shit had him off his game. Sam eyed Ian, *kept* his eyes on him, as he crossed the room and stood next to Noah. Then he did something unexpected and Ian's stomach flipped on end and sent beer shooting up his throat.

Sam fucking kissed the guy.

Ian sprinted to the bathroom. He had never been so damn happy to hang on a toilet rim.

*

"You okay in there?" Sam called from the other side of the bathroom door a minute later. Ian stood at the sink now, staring at himself in the wall-sized mirror. Wondering what the fuck just happened. What he had just seen.

You know what you saw.

Yeah, he knew. Fuck, he knew.

"Uh, yeah, I'm good," he answered, turning on the water even though he didn't need to just so Sam wouldn't freak out. The words were a big fat lie, but he knew Sam was a worrywart. Always had been. And Ian didn't want him or anyone else worrying about him. He finished up and opened the door.

"You sure?" Sam asked the second he stepped into the hall. "I thought you were gonna pass out."

"What? Oh, yeah. Nah, all good." He plastered on a fake ass smile. "Listen, about last night. I was fucked up. Forget everything I said. And did. Don't pay me any attention."

The half-naked douche making a fucking career out of scrambling some eggs and frying some bread watched them like a hawk and Ian raised a brow at him. Noah caught Ian watching him and turned away and Ian smiled. Fucking prick.

Sam took Ian by the arm and led him into the living room. "What's going on with you, Ian?" he asked when they were alone.

"Nothing's going on with me. I'm all good." Lie lie lie. "And I actually gotta get going. Got court today." More lies. Ian had no fucking clue when he had to be in court, but a way out was a way out.

"No. Don't leave yet." Sam's words and his sexy as hell voice always drove Ian crazy in the best way. The combo almost made him stay.

"Miss me already, huh?" He flashed a smile at Sam, who rolled his eyes.

"Disappear for a year and come back the same smug, conceited smartass you always were."

"You used to like my smart ass," Ian threw back with a grin. "Actually, you *loved* my smart ass if I remember right."

"Yeah, and you used to love *me*. Everybody changes a little, I guess."

Damn. He wasn't holding back.

"Stay," Sam said when Ian opened his mouth to say...what? "Yeah, and you loved me, too?" "I *still* love you?" "Go fuck yourself?" Shit.

Ian shifted his attention toward the kitchen. Naked Noah began setting out plates, his eyes trained on them. Ian shook his head. "Nah, not really into three-ways."

Sam slumped. "Jesus, Ian."

Ian said nothing, just stared at him. God, there were so *many* fucking things he wanted to say to him. How sorry he felt. How much he missed him. Still loved him. Wanted to change for him. "Sorry," he said instead, opening the front door. One word to cover a fucking world of screwing up. He nodded toward Noah, who still had eagle eyes on them, said, "Good luck with Kitchen Barbie," then pulled the door closed behind him.

Chapter Eight

Ian had no clue how he'd made his way back to Rachel's after walking out of whatever white-picket-fence shit Sam had going on, but he'd somehow managed to stumble to his bed and crash. He woke up hours later still sick to his stomach but headed for Final Draft anyway. Damned if anybody would say he wasn't consistent. The sun hung high in the sky and he did his best to stick to the shadows thrown across the ground by buildings and trees. Damn. He wished he'd waited until dark. Being out at night made him feel better because darkness hid flaws like makeup. And Ian needed lots of fucking makeup.

As he stood just outside the door to the bar, Ian's mind spun almost as fast as his stomach. And both made him want to hurl. Because of the beer. Because Sam had moved on. Because his life had become worse than shit. Everything sat in his gut like greasy Mexican food, thick and heavy and needing to get out. He knew he shouldn't be there since having a drink—well, a *fifth* drink, since he had downed four pints last night—could land his ass in jail, but seeing a guy at Sam's, the two of them living the life he had imagined would be his, *theirs*... Fuck, he just didn't give a damn anymore.

Jail.

Going on knowing Sam was with somebody else.

He struggled to see the difference.

"Fuck." He ignored the voice in his head telling him to go home or sit down on the curb and cry or step into traffic and fucking get killing himself over with already and opened the door. Touchy feely bullshit had never been his thing. Drown your emotions was so much easier, and what he did best.

He didn't want to be at Rachel's, sitting alone feeling sorry for himself. Avoiding your feelings is why bars were invented. Clichés were clichés for a reason, and none could be more accurate than misery loving company. He couldn't count on much, but if a bar opened for business, you could guarantee somebody would be saddled up, ready to drink until they didn't hurt anymore.

Some old man worked behind the counter and Ian wondered why Stacey wasn't there as he took a seat at the bar. Then he remembered the bright ass sun outside and figured the clock probably hadn't even struck noon yet and only losers like him started the day with a fucking drink. He didn't care though. Not enough to leave. Not after the shit he just saw. He ordered whiskey. Downed the shot. Another. Gone. Over. And over.

As his pain and embarrassment began a slow fade into the fringes of a drunken stupor, Ian couldn't get the image of Sam with another guy out of his head. Sam. With another fucking guy. Like being with somebody else was *normal*. Right. Sam should have waited. Ian had. Sure, he fucked guys. Even enjoyed fucking guys. But none of those guys meant a thing. Just sex. Not scrambled eggs and French toast and fucking cheesy ass smiles and kisses in the kitchen. Fuck.

More whiskey. More, more, more. Until asshat Noah wasn't shirtless anymore. Wasn't in Sam's house. In Sam's bed, fucking the guy Ian loved.

*

Several hours later Ian stumbled out of Final Draft. He stunk of beer and cigarettes and general Loser, if such a thing even had a smell. He knew it did. Loser smelled like him, his natural scent. Hell, maybe he'd corner the market on the fragrance. LOSER BY IAN. He'd be a fucking hit on Crack Alley and Skid Row, where everybody loved to shit on all the good in their lives so they wouldn't have to deal with anything real. He had already become the self-appointed president of the club; might as well earn a buck too.

His pocket started buzzing, and he almost broke his arm trying to dig his phone out. Sam was calling. He must have realized the gigantic fucking mistake he had made and wanted Ian back. Wanted *them* back. Like before.

Rachel.

"I'm fine, *mom*," he said after answering the call.

"I'm not your mother, Ian. Just checking on you, making sure you're not dead. Um... How'd things go with Sam last night?"

Ian took a beat. Heard what hid behind his sister's words. Laughed as realization set in. "You knew, didn't you? It's why you didn't want me to go. You fucking knew."

Several seconds of silence went by before she said, "Ian I am so sorry. Really. I didn't tell you because I didn't want to hurt you. I just—"

"So seeing for myself was supposed to, what, *not* hurt? Or were you just worried I'd get pissed off at you for being the one to keep me from making a fucking fool of myself?"

She stayed quiet again, then, "I just thought seeing Sam might help. Seeing him happy."

"Wow. Really fucked up, Rach. And are you serious? Happy? He's not happy. He's fucking miserable because he still loves me."

"Ian."

Ian shook his head. Got a few odd glares from strangers as he crossed town headed home. "No. I saw him. What was behind his eyes. He doesn't wanna be with a walking dick like Noah, Rach. He wants to be with me. Love me." He paused. "What we had? You only get a chance like ours once in life. And I..." *Fucked everything up* hung on his tongue but he bit back the words. Wasn't going there. He knew in his heart he was right.

"Ian, don't. You're only gonna get hurt if you do this."

"Jesus fucking Christ, don't you think I'm hurt already? Hurt is all I am now. Hurt is all I feel. And I'm fucking sick of feeling so damned hurt." He took some deep breaths and tried to slow the fucking merry-go-round he had jumped back on. "Sam's my way out of this," he said. "He is. I know he is. I just have to get him to see what I see."

"You can't—"

"*He will.* I'll make him see. Make him remember why he loves me."

"Really? How? What's your plan? Kidnap him? Keep him tied up in a basement somewhere until he says he loves you? You can't stay sober long enough to do anything."

Ian fumbled his way down Rachel's street—apparently a regular thing with him now—teetering between trees and picket fences and annoying ass people who didn't work for a living, so they spent their time jogging in the middle of the damn night and getting in his way.

"I'll stop."

Laughter from the other side of the call. Ian wanted to pull his sister through the fucking phone. "Get real, Ian," she said. "You're a—"

"I'm a what? A dick? Asshole? Fucking loser?"

"A drunk."

Ian stopped just short of opening the front door. Her words stung like a thousand bees. He liked to drink, yeah. And he knew he used alcohol to deal with the shit in his life, like most people who spent almost every night in a bottle or a bar. But he didn't think of himself as a fucking drunk. He hung up the phone and went inside. Rachel glared at him and tossed her phone on the sofa and got up.

"Really, Ian? Hang up on me?"

"You called me an alcoholic."

"I called you a drunk. There's a difference." She headed into the kitchen and started some coffee.

"Oh yeah? Do tell." Ian clipped the wall as he trailed behind her and did a three-sixty. The carousel topped out at full speed. Two glasses flew off the counter and exploded across the floor.

Rachel jumped. "Dammit, Ian! Stop. Don't move." She held out a hand toward him and went to grab a broom and dustpan from a tiny closet next to the fridge. "You wanna know what's different?" she asked as she swept up a million slivers of glass. "Functionability, for one."

Ian smirked. "Function-what? You're making up shit now."

"Alcoholics can still *function*. They have lives, jobs, families. Drunks—*you*—just stumble through life, breaking shit—"

"Fuck, Rachel, I'll buy you some more glasses."

Rachel dumped the pan full of broken glass into the garbage. "It's not about the glasses, Ian. It's..." she paused. "You know what? Never mind. You're drunk. You're not gonna remember anything I say anyway. Here, drink this." She pushed a steaming mug in front of Ian, who had somehow managed to plant his ass on a barstool across from her without breaking anything else.

"Smells good," he said, slipping a hand around the cup and inhaling the sweet aroma.

"Hazelnut," Rachel said, grabbing a bottle of water from the fridge. "Used to be your favorite."

"Still is. Shit it's hot." Ian smacked his lips and took another sip. He set the cup down on the granite countertop. "I..." He stopped talking. Stared at Rachel. Then past her, at the wall. At the sun beginning to rise, telling him he'd spent another fucking day drunk off his ass in a shitty bar. Those fucking emotions he had been trying to bury under beer and whiskey for the past year started clawing their way up his throat inch by painful, grating inch.

Rachel rested her elbows on the kitchen island. "What?" she asked. She watched Ian with such intensity. Watched his big brown eyes well up.

"I fucked up," he said after several seconds. He fought back tears. "I fucked everything up. I still love him. Miss him so fucking much." The tears won out, streaking his cheeks as they fell. "I *need* him."

"Ian," Rachel whispered as she went to him. She wrapped her arms tight around her brother and held him as he cried.

"God, I'm such a pussy," Ian said several minutes later. He pulled out of the hug and wiped his face. "Damn. Crying first thing in the morning will sober you up quick."

Rachel swatted away her own tears. "Then you should cry twenty-four-seven." She turned to the counter behind her.

Ian laughed. "Yeah, you're telling me."

"Here." She had the coffee pot in her hand and refilled his cup. "Drink up, Sunshine."

Ian picked up the mug. "Why?"

"If you plan on getting your man back, you're gonna need all the help you can get."

Chapter Nine

Ian had three days under his belt in his newfound sobriety. Three whole days. And he fucking hated every single second. Three days could be considered a personal record, yeah, but a record meant squat when he wanted to be even a little bit presentable for seeing Sam again. He had called him the next morning, halfway sober, and somehow managed to convince Sam to meet up with him, just to talk. Sam had agreed, which excited and panicked Ian all at once, and now today had come and he was full-on freaking the fuck out. He *needed* a drink.

"Ian!" Rachel's yelling made him jump and spill Jack Daniels down his bare chest.

"Dammit!" he yelled back. "The *fuck*!" He sat his tumbler on the kitchen counter and grabbed some paper towels to wipe himself down. "You scared the shit out of me."

"I said *no drinking*." She grabbed the glass and made a beeline for the sink. "You're not trying to get into a fraternity."

Ian scoffed. "Those dickholes don't have shit on me." He grabbed the bottle before she could pour the rest down the sink too. "Nope, nothing." He raised the whiskey over his head when she tried to rip the bottle from his hand. "Stop. I need it."

"Like a hole in the head. And Jesus, Ian, the sun's still up." Rachel gave up when he didn't back down and stepped away.

Ian lowered his arm and shrugged. "Sun's down somewhere."

Rachel rolled her eyes at him. "You also have to see your probation officer today. Are you *trying* to go to jail?" She held out her hand, and even though he wanted to turn the bottle up until he stared at the bottom from the inside, Ian gave up the battle and let Rachel win. She screwed the cap back on and Ian's chest tightened. "Please don't sneak off somewhere and buy another one," she added. "Don't drink. Okay?" Ian gave a half-assed nod. "And... Good luck."

Luck. Something Ian hadn't seen in a good while. Except the bad variety, of course. Bad luck always hung around. Hell, bad luck had been his best fucking friend. But he'd seen more than enough bad luck, thank you very much. High time he had some balance. Even if he had to fuck luck and get balance himself.

Which is why he needed Sam. For balance. Where Ian stayed high-strung, Sam stayed grounded. Crazy impulsive? Sam kept calm, thought things through. Balance helped them work so well together. The yin and yang shit or whatever. Sam the good to Ian's bad. A perfect fit. A perfect fit Ian had shit on.

But the past had to stay in the past. Today, he would fix everything. Fix *them*.

*

Ian knew he would have to work his ass off to get Sam back. And he'd have to start by apologizing for being such a dick the other night. God, he'd been such an asshole, showing up at Sam's drunk as hell. Coming on to him like some horny fucking teenager in heat. He should've just gone straight there like he'd planned. Like he'd told

Rachel he would. But... He'd been scared shitless to see Sam for the first time after all he had done—after walking out on him even though he'd wanted more than anything to stay with him forever—without some liquid courage. Turned out to be another fuck up on his part, surprise surprise. Now, he had to do some serious damage control.

He left the house and headed across town to the Paws for Life Animal Sanctuary. He hadn't seen or talked to him in over a year, not counting his ridiculous stupidity the other night, so he had no idea if Sam still worked there, but he'd bet his left leg he did. The man loved animals more than people and didn't mind saying so to anyone who asked. Ian had lost count how many times during their relationship they had pulled off the side of the road to help a turtle cross the street or check on what turned out to be roadkill to see if the bloodied mass could be saved. His love for animals fell somewhere on the list of a thousand things Ian found so attractive. His enormous heart always found a space for lesser creatures in need. Ian counted on Sam's compassion as he turned down a quiet side street just east of downtown.

A handful of mom-and-pop stores and a couple abandoned buildings lined the small hill leading to the shelter. Ian paid them no mind. Kept his head down as he walked by. Not because the neighborhood could be dangerous or anything. Hell, *no* neighborhood in this tiny town would ever be considered dangerous. He just didn't want to make eye contact and get stuck talking to somebody he knew but didn't care to see again. Plus, he wasn't what you would call proud to be home. He would rather die than have to explain to some random ass friend of his mom or dad why he never got married or had no kids or some other stupid shit people in this backwoods town considered "normal." Fuck no. He'd rather drink himself to death.

He walked up on the tiny porch spanning the front of the red and blue metal building and pulled on the door.

"Fuck," he mumbled and stepped back and took a peek in the dingy window to the right. The front office, if you could call a table and chair shoved in the corner an office, sat empty. He knocked on the glass and waited.

"We're closed for lunch."

Ian jumped. Turned around and saw Sam coming up from the left side of the building. His pale blue T-shirt hugged him so tight Ian's mouth watered. Sunlight bounced off his brown curls and smacked Ian right in the fucking face. Shit, he had to calm down before he did something he'd regret. Again.

"No problem," he said, stepping off the porch. "I was coming to see you, anyway." He headed to the far corner of the dirt parking lot, where Sam busily uncoiled a water hose from a hook on the wall. "You don't take lunch?"

"Not usually," Sam said, fighting the twisted hose.

"You, uh, need some help?" Ian asked, stepping up.

"I can handle a hose by myself."

Ian smirked. "Oh, you ain't gotta tell me."

Sam rolled his eyes. "What are you doing here, Ian? You left so fast the other morning I never thought I'd see you again."

Ian rubbed his neck. "Yeah, about the other night. I'm sorry. For showing up at your house out of the blue. Like I said, I was drunk and fucking stupid and..." He bit back the words *I wanted to fucking see you* even though they were desperate to get out. He would scare Sam off if he didn't ease up a bit.

"No worries," Sam said, getting the hose in line and dragging the heavy green rubber around the side of the building.

Ian followed. "No, I shouldn't have bothered you. I'd be pissed if somebody woke me up wasted and acting like a dick." He watched Ian dump a large metal bowl half-full of dirty brown water into the grass and rinse the inside out, the hose twisting in on itself again. "You sure you don't need some help?"

"I do this every day," Sam said. After some wrangling, he managed to get the hose to cooperate enough so he could fill the bowl. When he finished he added, "but if you feel like you owe me for the other night, having some help would be nice so I could get this done quick."

Ian smiled. "Whatcha need?"

"Here." Sam handed over the water hose and pulled a white cloth from his back pocket. "I'll clean them out, you fill them. Sound good?"

"Works for me."

Sam nodded and moved to the next pen. The large dogs, a couple of pit bulls, what Ian guessed was a chocolate lab, something mixed with who the hell knew what, spun in circles, jumping and barking as he cleaned out the two large bowls of old water. Ian stood back. He wasn't scared of dogs, but he wasn't as crazy obsessed with them like Sam either. And he remembered Sam telling him once how some of the dogs they got in had been abused and were territorial and sometimes violent, so he kept a safe distance just in case.

Sam finished wiping down the bowls and played with the dogs while Ian refilled them. He smiled as he watched Sam run back and forth while the pit bulls chased him, nipping at him like dog chow. The lab kept trying to knock him down, and the mutt did its best to lick him right in the face and Sam clearly loved every damn second. Ian's heart swelled because Sam seemed so happy. And Sam happy made *him* happy. Sad, too, because he missed this so much. Missed being happy with Sam. He hoped like hell he could fix the mess he'd made and get back to the good, happy place again.

"Don't be scared of them," Sam said when they closed the gate on the pen and headed to the next one. He breathed heavy, his chest puffed up from wrestling with the dogs, and sweat hung on his forehead. Sexy as fuck, in other words, and Ian got all glossy-eyed. "They come across as big and scary, but they're basically puppies trapped in adult bodies."

Ian laughed. "Yeah, I bet. You were sure having fun."

Sam wiped his forehead with the back of his hand and unlocked the next pen. Smaller dogs, terriers and shepherds and a collie or two, were bouncing around like balls the second they stepped in. "I love these guys," Sam said, reaching down and petting the ankle-biters.

"I remember."

"Yeah, guess you would know better than anybody." They stood there staring at each other as the dogs jumped and barked at them, desperate for their attention. But to Ian, he and Sam were alone. The dogs were gone. The pens and the shelter didn't exist. Only them. Together. Happy. "Earth to Ian." Ian refocused and saw Sam waving a hand in front of his face.

"What?" Ian asked.

"Where'd you go? Lost ya for a second there."

Ian shook his head. "Sorry. Guess I spaced out." No fucking way would he tell Sam he'd been imagining the two of them making out in the middle of a shit-filled dog pen.

Sam nodded to the water hose Ian held. "Want me to finish up?"

"Nah, I got this." Ian stepped toward the first bowl and water spewed from the hose while Sam cleaned out the second bowl at the other end of the long run of fence. The dogs followed him like sheep, waiting for him to pat their heads or rub their backs or play catch—which he did as soon as he finished. Ian moved down and filled the last bowl, then stood against the fence and watched Sam have the time of his life with half a dozen creatures nobody else wanted. Maybe hope would pay Ian a visit too.

*

They spent the next half an hour or so feeding and watering the rest of the dogs, laughing and getting along almost as well as they did when they were together, and to Ian the time felt like fucking heaven.

If he tried hard enough, he could almost forget he and Sam weren't *he and Sam* anymore. Almost forget he hadn't spent the past year or so drowning himself in drugs and alcohol but instead had been doing things like this— hanging out with Sam, enjoying life, spending all his time with someone he loved. With someone who loved him back.

But it wasn't reality. Not his anyway. No, his reality stayed full of broken promises and burned bridges. The biggest of which stood two feet from him. He owed Sam so much. The pain he'd caused, the worry—Ian's stomach turned just thinking about all he had put Sam through. He knew those were the reasons why he hadn't thought of any of this since the day he walked out on him. The one thing he had promised himself while he'd been gone? No matter what, he wouldn't think of Sam. Alcohol and drugs became the perfect blockers.

"Guess I better get back to work," Sam said once they were done cleaning up. "My boss will be back soon." He stepped up on the porch and unlocked the door.

"Yeah, I need to get going anyway," Ian said. He lied. He wanted to stay more than anything. He wanted to spend every damn second of the rest of his life with Sam.

"I... I had fun today." Sam stood in the doorway, one hand on the knob and the other crammed in his pocket. He seemed nervous, but in the best possible way. Like he had met a guy for the first time and wanted to impress him. Ian's heartbeat sped up.

"Me, too," Ian said, smiling. "Maybe we can do this again sometime?" Ian felt the way Sam looked, nervous as shit.

Sam hesitated a second before saying, "Uh, yeah, sure. I'm here every day. Just stop in whenever."

Ian smiled. "Cool, I will. Guess I'll see ya later then." Sam smiled back and went inside, and Ian exhaled the air he'd held hostage in his lungs. Jesus, why the hell had he acted like nothing had changed between them? Like he hadn't fucked things up so bad they didn't stand a chance of ever being fixed? He should be groveling at Sam's feet, begging forgiveness. Spending every second trying to make things up to him instead of not having the balls to even bring up the past. He was such a pussy.

Chapter Ten

A car pulled in as Ian skirted the lot, headed to the sidewalk. He dropped his gaze, shoved his hands in his pockets, and picked up the pace, in no mood to make small talk.

"Hey!" A man's voice, directed at him. Fuck.

Ian didn't acknowledge the voice. Didn't want to fake being happy to see somebody he hadn't thought of since he left town. He just wanted to get the hell out of there and get a drink to wash away some of the shame. "Ian, right?" Hearing his name grabbed his attention, and he stole a glance.

Fucking Noah.

Ian saw red. He wanted to kill the guy and didn't even know him. Didn't fucking matter. He couldn't stop seeing Noah's hands on Sam. His lips on Sam. His dick in Sam. The images drove Ian insane.

Noah walked up to him and held out a hand. Ian stared at the long, skinny fingers for a second. Thought how fast he could grab the hand and break every knuckle before Noah could get away. How easy he could make this guy suffer for touching Sam. He shook Noah's hand instead. The morning after his drunken visit to Sam he had been hung over as shit. And even though he saw quite a bit of the guy standing shirtless in the kitchen, he hadn't *really* seen him. Now stone-cold sober, Ian saw what he imagined Sam saw. Fucking killed him to admit, but Noah was hot, no doubt. Tall, well-defined, a man by definition. Made Ian hate him even more.

"Yeah," he said, staring Noah down.

"Noah. We met the other day?"

"Yeah, I remember. Uh, how are you?"

"I'm good, thanks." He glanced at the shelter. "So, um, what're you doing here? Thinking about adopting?"

Ian laughed and shook his head; he knew what the pretentious fucker was up to. "No," he said. "No time for a pet."

"Ah." Oh man, this guy. Ian smirked and waited, hoping the prick would say the right thing so he could lay into him. "Job hunting?"

Ian stared at him for a second. Couldn't believe he had the nerve to— "I don't think what I do or why I do it is any of your business," he said. "What *you* think?" Noah threw a jerk smile at him, and search the area again, like he wanted to make sure Sam wasn't watching before he showed his true colors.

"Uh, I think yeah. When it involves my boyfriend, what you do is definitely my business."

"Oh, so you tell Sam who he can and can't see or talk to, huh? That how things work between you two?" Ian's entire body pulsed, on edge, desperate to lash out and rip Noah apart. "Shit, now I feel bad for Sam."

"Do you? You feel sorry for him?"

"Real sorry for him."

"Funny, because he and I were just saying the same thing about you." Ian felt the punch to his gut. "Yeah, he went on and on about what a great, stand-up guy you used to be, and how now you're just so...sad. Depressing, even. He actually felt better when you bailed before breakfast the other day."

"Oh, did he?" Ian's hands were curled into fists. Fuck his probation. He'd be glad to sit in jail just to break this asshole's fucking nose.

Noah nodded. "He did," he said. "In fact…" he stepped closer to Ian, and Ian bit his tongue until he tasted blood. When Noah spoke again, his words were barely a whisper and soaked in attitude. "He said you kind of made him uncomfortable, and he wished you had just stayed gone."

Ian had no fucking clue how he managed to not beat the ever-loving shit out of the guy. Every cell in his body chanted, "Do it! Do it! Do it!" but for some reason he didn't. He stood there and let Noah have his moment. Let him bask in his fake glory, thinking he'd won and Ian would tuck his ego between his legs and slink away. No fucking chance.

"Well," he said, getting as close to Noah's face as he could without touching noses, "we just spent the past hour hanging out and he seemed pretty comfortable to me." They stayed eye-to-eye, nose-to-nose, for several seconds, so close Ian could feel the anger and rage coming off him. He could tell Noah wanted to lay into him as bad as Ian wanted to kick the shit out of *him*. Ian fucking wished he would just try.

But he didn't either. He stepped back half a step. Averted his eyes. Rubbed the stupid fucking hipster beard Ian wanted to rip from his stupid fucking face. "I know what you're up to," Noah said. "I know what your game is here."

Ian laughed and cocked a brow. "Do you?" he asked, crossing his arms over his chest. "Well, I definitely gotta fucking hear this. What's my game, man?"

"You think you're being slick. Slithering back into Sam's life like a hurt puppy needing a loving hand to nurse you back to health. But you're not fooling anybody. Not Sam. Sure as hell not me."

"I couldn't give two shits what you think about me, dude. Seriously."

"But you care what Sam thinks. And let me tell you, he doesn't think much. He knows what you're doing. What you're up to. And he's not falling for your crap."

Ian laughed. "You got some serious issues, buddy."

"I'm not your damn buddy."

"Damn right you're not. But you actually think I'm trying to worm my way into Sam's life by, what? Pretending to need his help to get my shit together or something?"

Noah smirked. "Like you would ever admit the truth."

"Oh, trust me, I'd have no problem admitting so if it *were* true. But it's not. No, truth is, I like Sam. Always have, always will. And not you or anybody else is gonna tell me I can't see him or hang out with him." Ian pushed this time, moving closer to Noah, lowering his voice. "And if it just so happens he starts wanting to be around me more than you, well, that's just gravy."

Noah full-on laughed this time. "God, you are something," he said.

"Thanks, man," Ian threw back, smiling.

"You honestly think you have *any* chance getting back with Sam?" Ian wanted to answer. Wanted to tell fuckface hell yeah, he did. He felt more confident than ever of his chances after the day he and Sam just had together. He kept his mouth shut instead. "You're pathetic."

Ian saw red again. "Call me pathetic again. Please fucking call me pathetic again."

Noah didn't back down. "What are you gonna do? Beat me up? Go ahead. I'm sure assaulting me will go over well with him. You'd be a shoo-in for sure." He laughed— he fucking *laughed*—and Ian had to conjure up every fucking ounce of his already weak self-control not to kill Noah right there in front of homeless animals. "Face the truth, Ian—"

"Don't say my fucking name, dude."

Noah paused a second and stared at him before adding, "You lost him. You had him, and you lost him. No, wait. You didn't lose him. You *walked out* on him. Threw him away like yesterday's trash. Now I've got him. And there isn't a chance in hell I'll give him up."

Neither of them noticed a car pull into the other end of the lot as they stood inches from each other hurling insults and innuendo. Or the lady in pastel-colored medical scrubs rubbernecking them as she got out and headed inside.

Ian smiled. "Don't worry, pal, you won't be giving him up. I'll be taking him back."

"Uh, guys? Is everything okay?" They both turned toward the shelter where Sam took careful, timid steps off the porch, headed in their direction. Ian backed away from Noah, who plastered on a fake fucking smile and walked toward Sam.

"Hey, babe," Noah said, taking Sam's hand in his and giving him a too-long kiss on the lips. He stared dead at Ian after he did and smiled and Ian wanted to bum-rush him and rip his head off his fucking shoulders.

"Hey," Sam said back, his eyes locked on Ian. "What's, uh... What's going on out here?" He kept his eyes on Ian for a second before giving Noah a smile. Ian held back a laugh because he knew Sam's was fake too.

"Oh, nothing," Noah said. Even his fucking voice changed when he Sam showed up. Like he had to fake *everything* so Sam wouldn't find out what a complete douche he really is. "Ian and I were just getting to know each other a little." Sam looked to Ian again. Those eyes. They were so full of worry mixed with fear. He was scared Noah was lying, Ian could tell. Seeing him so unsure...

"Yeah," Ian added, flashing a crocodile smile of his own. "All good." He swallowed back vomit and added, "You got a good one there, Sam." The words shredded his throat on their way out but the lie worked because Sam smiled for real and his shoulders relaxed.

"Yeah, he's okay," Sam said, slipping an arm around Noah's waist.

"Hey now," Noah said. He pulled Sam close to him and kissed the side of his head and Ian couldn't take another fucking second.

"You two... Later." Three words were all he could get out before his legs took over and dragged him down the street.

Chapter Eleven

By the time Ian's first visit with his probation officer rolled around, he felt unhinged. Three days without a drink, after not getting to make out with Sam or knocking Noah's nose off his fucking face, and he would have given his life to take the edge off. But he'd never get to do either of those things if he ended up in jail for failing a piss test. So, he steered clear long enough for the alcohol to clear his system and headed to town. Sam stayed on his mind, as usual. He tried to ignore him, focus on getting his shit together so he could win him back. Or at least try.

The PO's office definitely wouldn't be winning any awards. Sterile walls, sterile furniture, sterile people. The entire place stunk like dried shit and Ian's stomach roiled as he sat alone in a row of molded plastic chairs shoved under a large plate-glass window. A fake potted tree sitting in the corner probably hadn't been cleaned since someone stuck the ugly ass thing there a million years ago, shouting loudly for anyone who listened just how depressing the place could truly be. A chunky woman sat at a chunkier desk in the middle of the room, typing away on a late-model computer. Ian fixated on her to pass the time while he waited for his PO. He tapped a foot on the industrial carpet, his nerves coming alive. Fuck, he needed a drink.

"Ian Fisher?" A short man as round as he was tall stood in a doorway behind the woman's desk. Ian gave him a nod. "Follow me." They walked down a short hallway to the far end and into an office so bleak it made the main one seem like the fucking Taj Mahal. Ian's closet had to be bigger. Probably smelled better too. Jesus, apparently finding the oldest, moldiest buildings in the country for their agencies topped the list of fucking requirements for the US government. Ian's sinuses were flipping the hell out as his PO rounded the end-table-turned-desk and took a seat.

"Sit down," the man said, gesturing to a chair across from him. Ian did as the man said, figuring he'd be doing a lot of order-taking over the next few months. "I'm Mr. Walsh. I'll be your probation officer for"—he rummaged through a stack of papers and folders on his desk and plucked one from the bottom—"the next ninety days." He pulled a sheet from the folder, scribbled something on the bottom, and passed the paper over to Ian. "Sign this."

Ian took the paper. "Uh, what is this?" he asked.

"Your court order. What you have to do to stay out of jail. I need you to read and sign." Mr. Walsh never kept his eyes on the files on his desk as Ian poured over the rules he had to live by for the next three months of his life. No drinking. No drug use. Weekly visits to his PO with a piss test to make sure he didn't fuck up on the first two. He'd never been in trouble with the law before—how, he didn't know—so as far as he knew this list seemed standard. He'd cut down on his drinking, at least a few days before his appointments each week and steer clear of drugs. Rachel already said she would loan him the money to cover the court costs. He could do this. Being a Goody Two-shoes would suck, no doubt, but he could force himself for a couple months.

"Wait. Community service?" Fucking system, saving the worst for last. "I have *fifty hours* of community service?"

Mr. Walsh finally made eye contact. "I could recommend jail time instead. Your choice."

Ian shook his head. "Nah, this... This is good." This was *not* good. None of this was fucking good. Good would have been not getting in trouble. Not leaving home, or Sam, in the first damn place.

Sam.

"So, can I do these hours anywhere?"

Mr. Walsh pored over files again. Didn't bother paying Ian any attention. "Hours must be done at approved locations." He handed Ian another paper. "Here's a list." Ian gave the sheet a quick once over.

Shit. The shelter wasn't listed.

He dropped the paper on the desk. "Could I maybe work at the animal shelter on Lincoln? I know a guy there."

"Are they on the list?"

"Uh, no."

"Then no."

"So, I can only get credit for working at the places you say I can work? What does it matter?"

Mr. Walsh stopped working on whatever the hell had been more important and gave Ian his undivided attention. "Let me see if I can make this clear enough for you to understand. You were put on probation for a crime. Part of your probation is to complete"—he had to check the paperwork again; the man had the memory of a fucking peanut—"fifty hours of community service." He leaned back in his chair and clasped his hands in front of his big belly. "Now, you can do those hours at one of the places on the list, or you can go to jail. With the attitude you have, you're probably gonna end up there anyway."

"I don't—" Ian bit his tongue. Hard. This asshole... "Fine." He picked the list back up and slid the paper on top of the sheet of rules. "I'll check these out."

Mr. Walsh pulled himself back up to the desk and went to digging in files again. "Do what you want, Mr. Fisher. The choice is yours. My job is just to make sure you know the consequences of the choices you make." He reached into a box sitting on the floor behind him. Dug around for a bit before plucking out a tiny plastic cup with a green lid and tossing the container over to Ian. "Bathroom is directly across the hall. Fill the cup at least halfway. Don't flush the toilet. Come right back in here. Can you handle things on your own, or do I have to get up and watch you piss?"

Ian stood up. "I think I can manage." Fucking dick.

He did his business and brought the sample back to Walsh's office. The whole thing made him feel like shit. Having to check in with some random stranger every week, piss in a cup. He just wanted to get the fuck out of this prison without bars.

"We done?" he asked, setting the cup on the desk. Mr. Walsh opened his folder again. He peeled off a sticker with Ian's full name and a bunch of numbers emblazoned across the front from a sheet of paper in the folder and stuck the sticker to the sample. He jotted a few notes in the file as Ian stood in the doorway, itching to turn and run.

"Be here every Friday before five," Walsh said. "You miss a day, you go to jail. Fail a test, you go to jail. Get in any trouble over the next two months—"

"Go to jail," Ian interrupted. "Got ya."

Walsh gave a weak ass smile but looked more like he had been constipated for days on end. "See you in a week."

*

Ian cracked open a beer the second he got home. Yeah, he knew he shouldn't. He should give quitting a try instead, but if he didn't get a drink in him, he would go fucking crazy. His frustration over Sam and his dick boyfriend Noah and how much he wanted to kiss the former and punch the latter were overwhelming him. The second the icy brew hit his gut his nerves calmed down, and he relaxed. He leaned against the kitchen counter and savored every damn drop until the bottle sat empty.

"Really, Ian? It's not even noon." Rachel walked in and eyed him as she opened the fridge and started pulling out leftovers.

He belched and Rachel rolled her eyes. "Saw my PO this morning," he said. "Dick pissed me off. This helps me relax."

Rachel tapped the side of the empty beer bottle with her nail. "*This* is the reason you have a PO in the first place, moron." She grabbed a bowl from the cabinet by the fridge. "You hungry?" she asked as she pulled out a second one without waiting for an answer.

"I could eat." Ian plucked another beer from the fridge and took a seat at the island as Rachel popped open containers and started spooning out last night's spaghetti.

"What did he say?" Rachel asked.

"Who?"

Another eye roll. "Don't play dumb with me, Ian. Your probation officer. Is he nice?"

"Did you miss the part where I said he's a dick? No, he's not nice. He's a government asshole who thinks he's better than people on the wrong side of his desk. He's a fucking jerk. And why are you cutting the damn noodles up before you reheat them? That's fucking weird."

"What? It's not weird. They cut easier when they're cold. And don't try to change the subject." Rachel finished chopping up the spaghetti noodles in one of the bowls and drowned them in sauce. She slid the dish into the microwave and leaned against the counter while the bowl spun on the Lazy Susan inside. "Any surprises?" she asked.

"Got community service," Ian answered, taking a big gulp of beer. "Fifty hours."

"That's not too bad."

"Fucking sucks because I can't..." Ian stopped. He didn't want Rachel to know he'd been to see Sam at the shelter. And he really didn't wanna hear her shit.

"Can't what?" Rachel asked, pulling the steaming bowl from the microwave after the loud sequence of beeps. She gave the contents a quick stir with an oversized spoon and slid the whole thing in front of Ian. She got to work prepping the second one.

"Uh, I just... I can't fucking deal with this shit. Having to report to a fucking babysitter like I'm a child. So stupid."

Rachel put her own bowl in the microwave. "What's stupid is you getting in trouble in the first place. If you'd just—"

"Come on, Rach. Don't start in on me again, okay? I already know I fucked up. I don't need you reminding me every damn day."

Rachel threw her hands up. "Okay, okay. I'm sorry. I just worry about you."

Ian shoved a heaping forkful of spaghetti into his mouth. "Well don't," he said. "I'm a big boy. I can take care of myself."

"Don't talk with your mouth full, Ian. Geez, you're not five." Ian flipped her off and she shook her head. "And don't tell me not to worry. You're wasting your breath." She dropped her forkful of spaghetti back in the bowl. "Seriously, though. You sure you're okay?"

Ian rolled his eyes this time. "God. *Yes*. I'm fine. You worry too damn much."

"Sorry, not sorry." She finally took a bite of the marinara-soaked noodles she'd been toying with. "A worrier is just who I am." Ian made a goofy face and Rachel started laughing so hard she spit spaghetti across the counter.

And even though his day had been shit so far, Ian laughed too.

Chapter Twelve

It was official: Ian fucking hated doing community service. Not like he knew anybody who would *enjoy* having to do community service, but regardless, this sucked. A food bank had been the only place on his prick PO's list he thought would be somewhat simple work, but by the time he finished up his first day, he couldn't lift his arms. He had spent the past five hours hefting hundred-pound boxes of canned goods, taking them off shelves, loading them into trucks. He used to work out almost every day but hadn't been to a gym in God knows how long; every muscle in his body felt like they had been beaten with a meat tenderizer.

Sweat practically poured off him by the time the boss told him to quit for the day, and he headed home for a quick shower. Sam would be going on lunch in half an hour and he wanted to surprise him. He threw on some jeans and a T-shirt and grabbed the food Rachel had helped him put together before he'd left for "work." He had just shoved everything into a plastic bag, but she went behind him and repacked the meal in a basket like an actual adult. She should've used a fucking pink one to be less obvious, but her love still made him smile. He got to the shelter just as Sam locked up.

"Hey," he said, trying not to sound out of breath even though he had run almost the entire way.

"Ian, hey." Sam checked the door and stepped off the porch. "What're you doing here? I'm about to take a quick lunch."

Ian smiled. "Yeah, I know." He lifted the basket. "It's why I'm here. You hungry?"

Sam had a puzzled look on his face. "Did you pack a picnic?"

Ian dropped his arm. "Nah, Rachel did. I threw everything in a Walmart bag."

Sam laughed. "Yeah, that sounds more like you." He checked his watch. "Uh, I think—"

"I didn't bring anything special, just some sandwiches," Ian interrupted, holding up the basket again.

"Not...?"

Ian nodded and smiled. "Yep. Chicken salad with grapes and walnuts." Sam smiled and Ian forgot all about the pain shooting through every muscle in his body.

*

The park could've passed for closed, there were so few people out. Which surprised Ian given the fact the temperature had reached almost fifty degrees by noon. With so few days warm enough to be outside longer than fifteen minutes, he thought the place would be packed with people enjoying the heat wave. Or at least their lunch hours. He sure as hell was. Warmish weather, food, Sam by his side; the day had shaped up to be one of the best he'd had in months.

They found a spot next to a large oak tree and sat down. Small slivers of sunlight peeked through the thick branches overhead to keep them warm enough in the cool air. Of course, Sam being there, so close Ian could touch him if he wanted to, which, yeah, he fucking did, kept him plenty warm.

"Okay," he said, rubbing his hands together like Mr. Miyagi, "hope, you're hun—" Ian shut up the second he opened the basket. On top of the wax paper-wrapped sandwiches and bottled water sat a heart-shaped box no doubt filled with chocolates, along with a note reading, "be Sweet! Hahaha!" in Rachel's chicken-scratch handwriting. He could fucking kill her sometimes.

"What's wrong?" Sam asked, trying to peek into the basket.

"What? Oh, nothing." Ian yanked out the sandwiches and water and slammed the lid shut. He set the basket on the ground behind his back away from Sam. Things had been going well between them—well, since after the night he made an ass of himself—and he didn't want to scare Sam off with fucking heart-shaped candy. He already had a tough enough road ahead trying to figure out how to get Noah out of the picture. "Sandwich?" He handed one over to Sam and opened the other for himself.

"I haven't had one of these in forever," Sam said, taking a huge bite. He closed his eyes while he chewed. Even made the *mmm* sound people do when they eat something too good for actual words. To Ian, chicken salad was chicken salad. But watching Sam enjoy each bite, the way one corner of his mouth went up because he smiled and chewed at once, Ian fell in love all over again. Yeah, falling for a guy because of the way he ate a sandwich seemed corny as hell but Ian didn't care.

"Glad you like them," Ian said, smiling. "And glad you said yes. This is nice." The two of them having a picnic felt a bit weird, he had to admit, sitting on the grass eating like somebody out of a fucking fairy tale or something. But he didn't want to be anywhere else.

"Thanks for asking me." Sam put his half-eaten sandwich down and took a drink of water. Then he looked at Ian. "Hey, you remember the last time we were here?" Ian thought long and hard. He recalled something about being in a park late one night, drunk off his ass. He couldn't remember if he had been with Sam or off being a dumbass by himself.

"Uh...not really?"

"What?" Sam said with a laugh. "You forgot about the 5K we ran? When you got sick?"

"Oh, yeah," Ian said, laughing too when the memory came back to him. "Never been so fucking embarrassed." Well, not until the other night in Sam's front yard, which pretty much trumped everything else. "Man, I totally covered her feet." Sam laughed hard, the sound the best thing Ian had ever heard. He knew right then he always wanted to be the one to make Sam laugh.

"I had forgotten about her," Sam said, still laughing. "She was so ready to kill you."

"She wanted to, no doubt. I mean, the shit was chunky and everything."

Sam shook his head. "Oh God, don't. I just ate." They both laughed. "I told you not to eat before we ran but you wouldn't listen."

Ian shrugged. "Hey, I can't help I'm starving in the mornings. Some of us need food, you know."

"I need food," Sam said. "Just not the second I roll out of bed."

"Yeah, well, I didn't get sick because of the food." Ian leaned over and gave Sam a playful punch on the arm. "*Somebody* made me go out the night before."

"Oh, now it's my fault?" Sam glared at him but smiled. Ian could watch him smile all damn day. "Excuse me for wanting to celebrate my birthday with my boyfriend."

Hearing the word caught Ian off guard, like a punch to the gut. Boyfriend. It reminded him he once had Sam. They were once together. Until he had to wig the fuck out and destroy everything. And just as fast as his good time came, the almost-perfect moment disappeared. A heaviness settled over them like a storm cloud waiting to deluge them in the painful fact they were no more because of Ian. Sometimes he fucking hated himself.

He tried to salvage their good mood, chuckling at the memory, though the laughter felt forced. "I still had fun," he said, and even though he could see how uncomfortable Sam was, he smiled anyway.

"Yeah, me too," Sam said. "We used to have a lot of fun back then." Sam disappeared for a second, his eyes wandering. "I miss it," he finally said. "The fun."

Ian cocked a brow. "You don't have fun anymore?"

"No, no, I do. I just—I don't know. Noah is a lot different from you."

Fucking Noah.

Ian didn't know shit about the guy but hated him all the same. Hated him because he had been there when Ian wasn't. Hated him for stealing Sam. Hated him because Sam talked about him now and the distraction would ruin everything. Even though he wanted to jump ship and run before he said something he'd regret, Ian sat still. He couldn't imagine anything worse to talk about than Noah right then—or ever. But he and Sam were together. And what Sam wanted outweighed everything else.

"Uh…"

Say something. Say something. Say something.

"We can have fun."

Any fucking thing but that.

Sam stared at him and Ian could see in his eyes how much *he* wanted to jump ship and run. He opened his mouth to speak, but Ian shot him down.

"Jesus. Just forget what I said. I'm a fucking idiot."

"No, it's fine," Sam said, shocking the shit out of Ian. He just knew Sam would tell him to leave. Tell him he never wanted to see him again.

"You know I didn't mean anything 'untoward' as you would say," Ian said with a crooked smile. "I just meant we could hang out. If you wanted to."

Sam smiled back at him. "Thanks," he said. "Maybe."

A glutton for punishment, Ian said, "So, uh, how's he different?" He shook his head right after the words left his mouth, wondering where in the hell they came from.

They surprised Sam too. You would've thought Ian had asked him to fuck right there in the park. "Uh, well, Noah's a great guy. Really. Very sweet. Very attentive. I know he loves me."

Ian fought to not throw up the chicken sandwich he had just eaten. To sit there and listen to Sam go on and on about the guy taking the place in the life Ian should've had made his blood pressure soar and he wished he had packed a bottle of Jack with lunch. He wanted to do like he always did and drown out the noise with alcohol. Forget the fact the guy he loved, the guy sitting two fucking feet away, seemed to be in love with somebody else. Anxiety set in like concrete. Threatened to pull him under.

"But he's not very outgoing," Sam went on. "Kind of a homebody."

Ian swallowed the bile rising in his throat. Tried to keep his anger in check. Hoped like hell his rage didn't show when he said, "Didn't think you liked to party."

Sam shook his head as he stared at the river in front of them. "I don't. But I like doing other things. Movies, dinner, hanging out with friends. Just stuff, you know?" He looked at Ian. "You okay?"

Fuck no, he wasn't okay. Going in-fucking-sane described him better. "What? Yeah, I'm—I'm good." A year spent drunk and high, always hiding from the law and dealers he owed money to, taught him how to lie like a pro. "So, uh, why don't you tell him?" Jesus, what the hell was wrong with him? Something must have taken over his brain, his ability to think straight; no way in hell he'd keep talking about Sam's boyfriend on his own.

"Who, Noah?" Sam asked, as confused by what Ian said as Ian himself. "I don't know. I— It doesn't really matter, I guess. I mean, yeah, it'd be nice if we went out more, did more things away from the house, but I'm happy. I don't really need to."

Ian's skin crawled. His head spun. If he didn't get the hell out of there...

"I hate to cut this short," he said, standing up and grabbing the basket, "but I gotta go see my probation officer and I'm kinda already late." Another lie but he didn't care. He had to get the hell away from Sam and all the fucking talk about Noah and his superior greatness. And he needed a drink. Bad.

"Oh, okay," Sam said. He stood up and brushed grass and dirt from the back of his jeans. "I should probably get back anyway. Got a lot of work to do. I... I had fun."

Ian nodded. Tried not to meet Sam's eyes, see Noah there. "I, uh, I gotta go. I'll see ya later, okay?"

He heard Sam say, "Yeah, okay" as he walked away.

Chapter Thirteen

Ian sat at the far end of the bar at Final Draft. Four beers in already and he still felt like complete shit for leaving the park the way he did. When he showed up at the shelter and invited Sam to lunch, he had every intention of being nice and polite and not fucking things up again. He only wanted to spend time with Sam, get close to him again. Maybe convince him to come back to him. Love him like he used to. Then Sam started talking about Noah and how happy they were and...

"Fuck!" Ian slammed his hand down on the bar top and gripped the shit out of his glass of beer.

"Hey, watch yourself down there, Fisher. You break you buy." Stacey glanced at him from the other end of the bar and smiled as she settled the tab for a small group of underaged frat guys who clearly had already gotten drunk before even showing up; not even eight o'clock yet and they were shitfaced. Ian nodded to Stacey and stared at the Polo-wearing yuppies. They were cute, he had to admit. Hell, one of them even resembled Sam a little, but nowhere near as sexy. The way they kept flirting with Stacey and giving each other side-eye like they wanted to tag-team her couldn't have been a bigger turnoff but Ian didn't really care. He had zero interest in them or anybody else. He was horny as shit and had been since getting out of jail, but he would wait for Sam, the only guy he wanted.

The one guy he couldn't have. Which pissed him off even more.

"Can I get another?" he called out and tapped the bar. Stacey slung her rag over her shoulder and filled another mug from the tap. Ian downed the beer left in his glass just as she made her way over to him and set the full one on the cardboard coaster.

"What's got you in such a pissy mood?" she asked, grabbing the rag and giving the bar a wipe down.

"I'm fine," Ian snapped. "And Jesus, Stacey, enough cleaning. You trying to wipe the fucking color out of the wood?"

Stacey stopped and just stared at him. "Hey, watch your mouth, bud. Don't know who you're so fucking mad at, but it ain't me. Understood?" She didn't wait for an answer, which would have been a sarcastic nod of the head and a middle finger in the air, and went to help other patrons. Ian wanted to tell her, or anyone, why anger consumed him, made him so fucking upset. He needed to purge, get all the anger out of his system so he could refocus on getting Sam the hell away from Noah. But... He didn't have anybody to talk to. Not about this. Sure, he had Rachel, but all she would do is tell him to let Sam go, move on. And he didn't wanna hear her shit anymore. And Stacey wouldn't care even if he hadn't just pissed her off. He didn't have anybody else in his life he could go to with his problems. Not who he trusted. He had inadvertently cut ties with all of his hometown friends the day he left town and didn't talk to them again. And the one person he would turn to, the one person he *could* talk to without fear of rejection or judgment, was the very reason he got wasted all by himself.

Sam.

He and Sam used to talk about everything. If he'd had a bad day, or even a fucking awesome one, Sam couldn't wait to hear every detail and give advice or praise. Hell, he even seemed interested in Ian's life, like he cared and wasn't just pretending like so many people had before. And Ian did the same for him. Anytime he came home from the shelter with stories of a dog being abused or adopted, Ian gave his undivided attention. He would hold him close and let him cry out his pain when they had to put one down. He even got just as excited as Sam did when Sam had found one a good home. They had a fucking *life* together. With ups and downs and good and bad, they took together in stride, supporting each other and being there for each other. They had the kind of life Ian had always wanted.

"So why the fuck—" Ian stopped himself when he realized he had spoken out loud. Checked to make sure no one overheard him. The place wasn't too busy for a Friday night, though the bars didn't really get packed until after midnight, still a few hours away. If he sat there long enough, the place would no doubt fill to the brim since Final Draft held the distinction of being the only bar in town worth a shit. He closed his eyes and tried to block out the noise from the bar and in his head. Block out the fact he had managed to fuck up his life in epic proportions. Sam's life too, he had no doubt.

He couldn't help but laugh. He'd had everything. And lost everything. No, "lost" wasn't right. Wasn't the truth. He didn't *lose* anything. He knew all along where his happiness had been. The happiness he would give anything to have now. With Sam. His happiness had been with Sam. And Sam's happiness had been his. And he fucking *let* everything go. Hell, things would have been easier to swallow had he *actually* lost everything somehow, by Sam cheating on him or just not loving him anymore for whatever reason or something. But no, he didn't get the easy way out. He didn't get to sit there feeling sorry for himself because he lost everything he had ever wanted over something he couldn't control. He chose to walk away from Sam of his own free will. Nobody made him. Sam hadn't given him an ultimatum. Nobody held a fucking gun to his head. He had the choice to stay or go, and he left. Just. Fucking. Left.

He balled one hand into a fist so tight his bones hurt and downed his fifth beer with the other. He wanted to drink until the bad shit went away.

*

Ian stumbled out of Final Draft an hour later feeling pretty good, just sloshed enough to not feel the pain which had taken hold of him since the second he got back into town. Since he first saw Sam again. He had climbed back on the familiar merry-go-round, spinning fast enough he couldn't make out the images flashing in front of him. Which is exactly how he liked to be, too drunk to give a damn.

He did his very best to hold on to the fraction of clear thought he had left as he headed home. He didn't want to have to try and explain to Rachel or anybody else a broken bone or skull fracture from face-planting on the sidewalk. He crossed the street a block down from the bar and headed east. The crowd thickened as he got closer to the shops and restaurants, people moving in and out of the storefronts, living their lives. He couldn't believe the streets were so busy so late at night. He felt jealous of all of them because they were doing what he wanted to be doing, moving on, but couldn't. He couldn't move on from Sam. Sam held too tight a hold on his heart, his soul. Moving past him wasn't an option.

He tried his best to avoid bumping into anybody, throwing a smile and a "sorry" if he did. A trio of girls held him up when he almost sideswiped one of them. They were laying on the flirting so thick even Ian could tell and he was beyond wasted. He smiled, chatted them up, forgetting for a minute about Sam and his jacked-up life. He kind of felt...good. Which should have been a big red flag.

"Ian?" He heard the voice above the giggling girls and general din of the busy street. He glanced over his shoulder, and the smile and good time he'd been having with perfect strangers vanished.

Sam. *With Noah.*

Ian stared at them like a deer in headlights before saying good-bye to the girls—the redhead shoved something in his pocket Ian figured had to be her phone number—and walked over. Why, he had no fucking clue. He had zero fucking desire to see Sam with Noah. Again. The morning at Sam's house had been more than enough for a lifetime of nightmares. But he did, anyway. Even plastered a fake smile on when he reached them.

"Hey, you two," he said, giving each of them a friend-zone pat on the shoulder. He stumbled a little and Sam reached out to stabilize him but stopped. Pulled his hand back. Turned to Noah and smiled. "What brings you two lovebirds out tonight?"

"Dinner," Noah answered. Ian locked on Noah's eyes and saw the anger there, the rage he tried to keep in check. Yeah, Ian felt the same fucking way. Inside, he felt like a volcano bubbling up, ready to erupt.

He kept his shit together and smiled. "Nice," he said. Focused on Sam this time. "I see you got him out of the house. 'Bout time, huh?"

"What did he just say?" Noah snapped. Ian noticed Noah's grip on Sam's hand tighten. They were fucking holding hands, like the two of them together had to be the most normal thing in the fucking world. "Sam, what the hell did you tell him?"

"Nothing," Sam threw back. Ian smiled like a mischievous kid who had just pulled one over on the babysitter. Which he kind of was. And he knew it. He knew how to be a major dick. He just didn't give a damn at the moment.

"Uh oh," he said, "Did I get somebody in trouble?" His eyes were on Sam's, and even though he passed drunk a long time ago and had zero chance of remembering any of this tomorrow, he would never forget what he saw in Sam's eyes.

Disappointment.

"Screw you, Ian," Sam spat out. He let go of Noah's hand and got right up in Ian's face. "I don't know what your deal is but go fuck yourself." He stepped back, took Noah's hand in his again, and turned to walk away.

"I'd rather you screw me!" Ian yelled after them. They didn't stop, but Noah threw him a this-isn't-fucking-done glare over his shoulder and Ian mock-saluted him and flipped him off.

Shit. He just didn't know when to quit sometimes.

Chapter Fourteen

Someone had once told Ian he could compare his life to a giant hamster wheel. You run and run and run, but never get out of the loop until you die. Another morning waking up hungover and full of regret, and he started to understand.

He fucked up again. He should get a T-shirt made, have those words etched onto his damn tombstone, because fucking up had become his mantra. Screwing up his life when things were going right seemed to be the only thing he had ever been good at, to be honest. Not that the shit with Sam had been right by any means, but things were a million percent better than they were a year ago when he had walked out. When he had tucked his sad tail between his legs and ran away to bury his problems with drugs and alcohol. He and Sam had been getting along. Starting over. And Ian knew Sam felt...something again. Not love, maybe. Not yet. But the feelings he'd had for Ian were coming alive again, Ian could tell. So of course, he had to open his fucking mouth and stomp on all the progress he had made.

He felt like a mindless, soulless zombie as he pulled himself out of bed and took a shower. Got dressed. Went downstairs and made coffee. His head throbbed every time his heart beat, so he took a few aspirin for breakfast. No way in hell he would risk eating anything more substantial. The way his stomach felt he'd be hosing down the kitchen in vomit if he did. He sat there nursing his cup of coffee, trying to figure out a way to fix the fucking mess he'd made.

"Wow, you look like death," Rachel said when she bounced into the kitchen like she'd just won the fucking lottery. A ponytail swung behind her, something she *never* did, and she smiled as she filled her own cup.

"Thanks," Ian said with a sarcastic nod. "What the hell's gotten into you?"

She finished adding cream and sugar to her cup and blended them all together. "This is kind of our thing now, huh? Hanging out in the kitchen every morning, talking about life. Feels nice." She smiled and took a sip. "Mmm, so good. Great job, little brother."

"Holy shit. Were you abducted by aliens or something last night? You're acting really fucking weird."

Rachel smirked. "*Or something,*" she said.

Even in his hazy, hung over state, Ian picked up what she had dropped. "Son of a bitch. Did you get laid? Jesus, Rach, you're still fucking married!"

"Calm down, *Padre*. I didn't have sex last night. And I'm not still married. Well, technically I am, but only because Chris and I don't have the money to—never mind. Doesn't matter. My point is, I didn't do anything wrong."

Ian laughed. "Shit. You know how many times I've used that line? And how many times I *always* did something wrong?"

Rachel rolled her eyes. "Whatever."

He took a sip of his coffee. Let the warm liquid slide down his throat, maybe help sober him up even a little. "Okay spill," he said. "He have a big dick?"

"Jesus, Ian!" She dabbed at her shirt after almost choking on the mouthful of coffee she half spit out. "God, could you be any more crass?"

"Crass?" Ian said, raising a brow. "You the queen of fucking England now?" She didn't answer, so he added, "What did you do, bag a professor?"

"Oh my God, you're impossible." She grabbed a dishcloth from the sink and dabbed at a spot of coffee on her shirt. "Great, now I have to go change."

"Nuh-uh, not yet." Ian snapped his fingers at her. "Not till you tell me what has you acting like a fucking fifties' housewife this morning. And don't try to pretend it's not a guy. I'm hung over, not stupid."

Rachel set her coffee cup in the sink. "Well, even though my, um, *personal* life is none of your business, while you were out doing whatever made you wake up like *this*"—she wagged a finger at him—"I was on a date." She stuck her nose up in the air and smiled, and Ian laughed. "What's so funny?" she asked.

He shook his head. "Nothing." He smiled ear to ear when she popped him on the arm. The banter between them. She acted like he had never hurt her by leaving like he had Sam. He hoped Sam would find a way to be as forgiving as his sister.

"So, what's up with you?" she asked. "Why are you acting like somebody stole your favorite shirt?"

"Favorite shirt? Really?"

Another eyeroll. "You know what I mean."

Ian shrugged. "Not much," he said. "Just fucked myself. You know, the usual."

Rachel nodded. "Well you must enjoy it. You certainly do it enough." Ian gave her the finger. "And there's another thing you do a lot, smart ass. I just mean you tend to gravitate toward drama. That's all."

"Oh, well, good to know." Ian got up from his seat and finished off the coffee in the pot. He stood next to Rachel and took a giant sip. "I don't know what's wrong with me," he said. "I keep screwing up everything good in my life."

Rachel's face softened, and she gave his shoulder a comforting squeeze. "Don't put yourself down, Ian. You're a great guy. You just make bad decisions now and then." Ian rolled his eyes at her. "I mean it," she went on. "You kind of don't know how to get out of your own way."

"What the hell do you even mean?"

"I mean stop overthinking everything you do," she answered, moving to the fridge to grab some water. "Trust yourself to make the right decisions. And don't get so upset when you screw up. I'm sure things are never really as bad as you make them out to be, anyway."

"I ran into Sam and Noah last night. And basically told Noah Sam and I spent the day together."

Rachel clutched her bottle of water to her chest. "Aww, you guys did? I'm so happy for you, Ian."

"Missing the point there, sis," Ian said.

Rachel cocked a brow. "Am I?"

"Uh, yeah."

Rachel walked back over to him and put a hand on his crossed arms. "Hey," she said, staring up at him. "This is what I mean about getting out of your own way. So, you slipped up and said something you shouldn't have. So what? You and Sam hanging out wasn't for nothing. I assume you had a good time?"

Ian shrugged. "Yeah, I guess. Till he started talking about Noah and how happy he is."

Rachel thought a minute about what he said. "Okay, so, things didn't go *exactly* how you probably wanted, but all went well otherwise?" Ian nodded. "Then hold on to *that*, and not the part where you screwed up. Maybe then you won't get so upset." She glanced down at her watch. "Crap, I gotta get going. Call me if you need me, okay?"

"Yeah."

She smiled at him. "Chin up, baby brother. Life won't suck forever. I promise."

"Jesus, you need to quit dating. I can't handle this much positivity so early in the morning."

"Screw you!" She smacked his arm again, and he laughed.

"There she is. There's the sister I know and tolerate." Rachel threw a middle finger toward him as she left the kitchen. Ian smiled and shook his head and finished off his coffee.

Rachel could be a fruit loop sometimes, and clearly her wacky side amped up by about a thousand when she met a guy she liked, but maybe she had been right. Maybe things weren't as bad as he thought they were. Maybe he hadn't screwed up his chances of getting Sam back.

"Only one way to find out," he said aloud, dropping his mug in the sink and heading upstairs.

*

He walked up to the shelter just as they were opening for the day. A cute woman with short-cropped hair and kind eyes greeted him when he walked in.

"Hi," she said. "What can I help you with today? Here to get a new friend?" For a second Ian thought she meant herself until he remembered they were in the job of finding homes for the animals they housed and had to choke back a laugh.

"Um, actually I'm here to see Sam? He busy?"

The woman smiled at him. "Oh, are you Noah? He's told us so much about you." She picked up the phone and started pressing buttons. When she spoke again, her voice boomed through the entire building. "Sam you have a visitor at the front desk." She replaced the receiver. "Very nice to finally meet you."

"I'm not Noah," Ian said. His blood pressure rose, and he had to force a smile. "I'm an old friend of Sam's. Just stopped in to say hi."

"Oh." He could tell he had made her uncomfortable, which kind of made up for her being a total idiot and mistaking him for a douche. "Well, you're welcome to have a seat. Sam should be up in just a moment." Ian faked another smile, and she faked one right back. He made a note about the lesson of judging a book by the cover as he took a seat to wait for Sam.

He flipped through a few of the outdated magazines stacked on a small table next to his chair, his nerves fighting to get the best of him. He refused to let them win, focusing instead on the fact he and Sam—before he fucked things up, of course—were in a good place. And he planned to make sure they ended up there again.

"Ian?" Sam said as he came through a large, windowless door behind the receptionist's desk. He stopped the second he saw Ian sitting there. Cut his eyes at Miss Congeniality. "What are you doing here?"

Ian could see, written all over his face though he tried hard to appear happy, Sam had hoped for somebody else. Anybody else. He felt like less than a piece of shit but stood up anyway. "I was wondering if we could talk." He had his hands stuffed in his pockets so Sam wouldn't see them shaking. Fucking nerves.

Sam let the door shut behind him and stepped closer. "Uh, yeah, okay," he said. "Let's go outside." He opened the front door and Ian followed him out like a scolded dog. "So, why are you here, Ian?" Sam had his arms folded over his chest and a sour expression on his face. He damn sure didn't intend to make this easy.

Ian stared down at his feet for the longest time, praying to God or *the* gods or the fucking wizard of Oz or anybody who would listen to give him the courage to speak. "I came to apologize," he somehow managed to say. "Again."

Sam gave a little laugh. "You're becoming a pro at saying sorry."

Ian smiled. "Maybe I should write a book." Sam wasn't amused so Ian moved on. "I am sorry, Sam. I never meant to tell Noah or anybody anything you told me. Or have ever told me. I... I broke your trust. I just wanted you to know I didn't intend to do anything to fuck things up for you two. Honestly. I was drunk and—"

"This excuse is kind of getting old," Sam interjected. "You might want to start thinking up a new one."

"You're right," Ian agreed. "But I'm not making an excuse. What I did was wrong. I acted stupid and childish, and I regret what I did."

"Really? Because you sure seemed like you were enjoying yourself. You looked kind of proud to me. Like you thought Noah and I would maybe break up because of what you said." He eyeballed Ian. "So, did you?" he asked. "Did you think you would run back to Noah and tell him, and he would dump me?"

"What? No, Sam. Of course not. I—"

Sam shook his head. "Save it, Ian. You crossed a line last night." He paused and stared at Ian. "I—I think maybe we should not see each other for a while. At least until I can smooth over the mess you made with Noah."

Ian's heart sank down to his feet. He felt dizzy like he would drop any second. "Sam, please. Don't."

"I'm sorry," Sam said, and Ian could see he meant those words. Which hurt even more. Sam didn't want to cut him off, but Ian had left him no other choice. Because he had to open his fucking mouth, Sam had been forced to choose. And he chose Noah. "I gotta get back to work." He stepped past Ian and onto the porch. He turned back just before going inside. "Ian?" Ian spun around. Sam lowered his eyes a second. "Please do this," he said. His eyes were full of so much pain. Ian's heart shattered. "For me?" He didn't wait for an answer and went inside, leaving Ian to pick up the pieces of his shattered world all by himself.

Chapter Fifteen

Ian somehow found the strength to stay away from Sam for a full week. Not being able to talk to him or even see him just about killed Ian, but he pushed through. And since he had to report to the principal every fucking Friday like a kid in detention and couldn't piss alcohol, he spent the first half of the week wasted, slumming around the house doing jack shit. He did knock out the community service hours he had left, though, so his time alone wasn't a total wash. He put in as many hours as they'd let him until he finally got a signed form saying his court-ordered days as free labor were paid in full. One less thing to worry about, which was good because he had plenty on his mind. And by plenty he meant Sam, and the fact he pulled away every time Ian saw him. Ian ended the fasting period with a probation visit Friday just before they locked up for the weekend. He paid his monthly fine, pissed in a cup, and got the hell out of there.

He had zero plans to swing by Final Draft, but the place called out to him. Three days sober—he'd be so fucking glad when he finished his probation so he could drink whenever the hell he wanted again—and his spidey senses kicked in, seeking out alcohol. He made a beeline for the bar and plopped a twenty on the counter.

"Keep 'em coming," he said. Stacey worked behind the counter again, which always made him smile. She made her way down to him with a tall glass of his salvation.

"You still in a bitchy mood?" she asked. "Or have you grown up since the other night?"

Ian downed half the glass. "Not a chance," he answered. "And I'm always in a bitchy mood. You're just the lucky one who hardly ever sees it."

"Oh yeah. Lucky." She smiled and took his money and added the bill to a pouch on the apron tied around her waist. Ian waved a hand at her and kept drinking.

Stacey did as he asked and kept a full glass in front of him even after his money had no doubt dried up. She had always been good to him—or bad, depending on who you asked—which explained his love for the woman. Strong as hell, takes no shit off anybody, and somehow managed to put up with his ass; if he were straight, he would've already asked her to marry him. He watched her work the entire bar, in front of and behind, like a pro. She bussed tables, mixed drinks, and flirted just enough to pad her pockets. All the while making him feel like the only person in the place who mattered. She always knew just what he needed.

"You want another, or you about done?" She came back over just as his buzz began to ebb, wiping the counter like a machine with the white towel she always had in hand.

"Damn, is cleaning like a fetish for you or something?" Ian asked. "And yeah, one more."

Stacey cut her eyes at him and went to fill another mug of beer for him. "Last one," she said as she set the foam-topped delicacy in front of him. "Your twenty is tapped out." She gave him a wink and he smiled.

"You're too good to me," he slurred, polishing off one beer before starting in on the next one.

"Oh, I know." She dropped the empty mug into the bin under the counter. "So, what's going on with you, Fisher? Something's been off the last couple times I've seen you."

Ian took his time with his beer, his last one, relishing the feeling alcohol gave him. He craved the numbness, the mindlessness you could only find at the bottom of a bottle. Or a frosty mug. "My life is shit," he answered. "Keep screwing up every chance I get."

Stacey gestured to the room and laughed. "Welcome to the club, my friend."

Ian smirked. "Yeah. Jury of my peers."

"Nope. No judgment here. This ain't a church."

Ian laughed. "Shit. A church would burn to the ground if I walked through the doors. Kinda surprised this place hasn't done the same."

"You kidding? This bar was *built* on sinners. And a few who thought they were saints. We welcome the poor, the tired, yada yada." She rested her elbows on the bar across from him. "Hey," she said, nudging him. He took a couple seconds, but he managed to focus on her face. "Quit shitting on yourself, you hear me? You're a great guy. A catch, as they say. Things'll turn around for you soon."

"Obviously you don't know me as well as you think," Ian said with a crooked smile. "I'm no fucking catch."

"Trust me, Fisher. You are."

Ian sat silent, staring her down. Waited for the joke. When the punchline didn't come, he slumped back in his seat. "Uh, thanks, Stacey. You're...sweet?"

Stacey smirked and stood up and went back to trying to wipe off the lacquer on the bar. "You repeat what I said, and I'll cut your tongue out." She winked at him and walked away.

Ian sat there and nursed his last beer, thinking about what Stacey had said. He sure as hell didn't feel like a catch. A beer-guzzling, unemployed loser whose only talent had been wrecking everything in his path didn't tend to go over well on Scruff or Grindr or any other app some bored preppie too smart for his own good created so people could find nearby fucks but still hate themselves in private. Still, Stacey was important to him. And if she felt he had some sort of redeeming quality buried deep... Maybe he should start believing her? Who knows, maybe things would start to turn around for him soon.

He upended the glass, dropped another ten bucks on the bar, and left.

*

Ian hoped one day he would learn from his mistakes. Unfortunately, today wouldn't be the day. Nope. If Judgment Day had been upon him, he would've gone straight home and crashed. Nursed a hangover the next morning without regrets, like any normal red-blooded American. And he couldn't be farther from normal.

He had heard every single word Sam said to him last week outside the animal shelter. Sam had asked Ian to give him space. To not see him for a while. And Ian had. He gave Sam a week, which turned out to be six days longer than he had expected to do as told. But even God himself rested on the seventh day so why shouldn't Ian get the same break? The answer stretched out for a fucking mile, and Ian was way too drunk to pore over the list of reasons why he should stay away from Sam until Sam came to him. So, he let the booze take over like he always did, and he knocked on Sam's door in the middle of the night again before he could stop himself.

He kept a hand on one of the posts flanking the steps of the porch to keep from falling over while he waited for Sam to come to the door. Any other time he would've talked himself out of doing something so stupid, would've told himself making such a huge fucking mistake would only make things worse. But he wasn't in charge of this mission. The umpteen beers he drank were. And they wanted him to see Sam *now*. He leaned forward to knock again just as the door swung open.

"Ian?" Sam whispered, stepping out onto the porch and pulling the door shut behind him. "Seriously? What the hell are you doing here? I asked you to give me some time."

"I did," Ian said, stumbling backward. Sam reached out and grabbed his arm. "A whole week."

Sam huffed in frustration. "Jesus, Ian, I didn't mean give me a couple of days. I meant... Give me as long as I need to process everything."

Ian's brow furrowed. "Process what? What's there to process? I fucked up. Made a mistake. I apologized. So just forgive me already so we can hang out again."

"You know nothing is ever so simple. There's a lot more going on here than just you and me hanging out." Sam's words confused to say the least. He only heard about half of what Sam had said thanks to being beyond intoxicated, which made what Sam hinted at harder to process. Sam took off his glasses and pinched the bridge of his nose. "Shit, you're so drunk I'm probably wasting my breath here."

"No," Ian said, putting a hand on Sam's shoulder. "No, you're not. I promise. Yeah, I'm kinda fucked up right now, but I'm listening. I swear."

Sam exhaled. "I know you still love me," he said. Ian smiled. "And...God...I'd be lying if I said I didn't feel *something* for you too. How could I not? We were together for over three years, Ian. Of course I still care about you. I always will. But what I feel doesn't—"

Ian put a finger to Sam's lips. "Don't," he said. "Quit trying to ignore the fact you still love me too."

"I didn't say love."

"You didn't have to. I can feel it." He let go of the post and used Sam for support. They were close enough he could smell Sam's body wash and the scent made his head spin more than the alcohol. "I know you can too."

"Ian," Sam said, backing up. "Please." Ian stopped advancing but didn't let go of Sam's hands. "Listen," Sam went on. "You have to back off, okay? I don't know what I'm feeling or not feeling right now. It's the middle of the night and I'm tired. I just wanna go to bed. We can talk about this later."

"When's later?" Ian asked. "Tomorrow? Next week? Next fucking month?"

"I...I don't know. I'm sorry."

Ian let go of Sam and leaned against the post behind him. "Sam, please. I can't go day after day, over and over, without seeing you or talking to you. I *need* you. In my life, I mean. I need you in my life." He had a sudden burst of clarity amidst the drunken haze and knew Sam *had* to be freaking out. "I've missed you so much. Missed us being in each other's lives. I just want us back. That's all I meant."

"I know," Sam said. "And I do too. I just—"

"Don't 'just' anything," Ian interrupted. "Don't overthink this or talk yourself out of what's happening. Just fucking go with the flow." He pushed Sam against the door and kissed him. Hard. His tongue invaded Sam's mouth, probing, desperate to taste every part of him. He gripped Sam's neck, pulled him into the kiss. Pulled their bodies together. Waited for Sam to kiss him back.

He didn't.

Sam pushed Ian, hard, knocking him into the wall and down to the floor.

"Dammit, Ian," he snapped. "Why are you like this? Just do whatever the hell you want, no matter who gets hurt?"

"Hey, I'm the one on the floor here, not you." Ian rolled over and got on all fours. The ground spun like a kaleidoscopic top under him and he swayed back and forth.

"God, you're fine. I wish you would just listen to me."

"I'm listening, I'm listening." A total lie. Trying to get up off the porch left no room in his brain to zero in on what Sam had said. "A little help?" He lifted a hand into the air, hoping Sam would take the hint and pull him up. He didn't.

"Go home, Ian," Sam said. "And please don't come back." Ian faced the ground when he heard the door slam shut behind him.

Well, things definitely did not go like he had hoped.

Chapter Sixteen

Ian summoned every ounce of strength he had left to drag himself home last night. Sure, the alcohol hadn't helped. Or the fact he might have cracked a damn rib when he hit Sam's porch. But what sucked all the air from his lungs, punched him hard in the gut, left him wanting to do it all over again, was the kiss.

Their fucking kiss.

Even though Sam didn't kiss him back, Ian had been over the fucking moon excited when he got to feel those lips he had missed so much against his own. The past had come rushing back in those few seconds, flooding his mind with memories of the first time they kissed. Said kiss happened on Sam's twenty-first birthday, at Final Draft. Ian had been drunk then too, but lust outweighed the booze and he and Sam made out like crazy. Last night might not have been as long of a session, but for Ian the kiss felt just as momentous.

He crawled out of bed and got dressed with a smile, an actual fucking *smile*, on his face despite the hammering going on in his head. The first time in...shit, he couldn't even remember, he had woken up with promise about the future. Not since his parents' deaths, he knew for sure. No, the last time had been with Sam. Sam had always made him smile, even when life had gone to shit. Sam's laugh. The sexiest dimples God had ever put on Earth. The way he smelled after a shower, all fresh and clean and delicious. Ian was nothing *but* smiles when he and Sam were together. And he fucking missed feeling so good.

The past year had been dark and smile-less, if that was even a word. But now, things were beginning to turn around. Even if Sam refused to admit his feelings for Ian, railed against them. He could push Ian away all he wanted, but no a chance in hell Ian would give up.

*

"Wow, somebody's in a good mood." Rachel came into the kitchen a few seconds after Ian and made a beeline for the coffee pot. The room grew heavy with the earthy aroma of fresh ground beans seconds later. "Guess last night went well?"

"Better than well," Ian said. He chose to ignore how things had ended between him and Sam, focusing on the good instead of the bad. Progress was progress, no matter how warped. He plucked a banana from a basket of fruit sitting off-center on the island, broke open the peel, and bit off half. "He still loves me."

"Don't talk with food in your mouth, dummy." Ian flipped her off and inhaled the rest of the banana. "Did he actually *say* he still loves you?" Rachel went on. Ian picked up on the hesitation and doubt behind her words.

He grabbed another banana and repeated the process. "Not exactly," he said, though *not at all* would have been more accurate. "But he does. I know he does."

"Ah, you know, huh? Somehow you just *know* he still loves you even though he's with somebody else? *Living* with somebody else?"

"He kissed me."

Rachel stopped spooning sugar into her coffee and turned to face him. Ian nodded and raised a brow.

"A good kiss too," he added. "So fucking good. Like, *holy shit* good." He got up from the bar and tossed the banana peels into the trash. "So, no, he didn't have to say anything."

"Ian, don't—"

He held out a hand at her. "Nope, don't even start. You're not gonna ruin my natural high." He went to the fridge and grabbed a water, wishing his sister had beer because he could have fucking used one to deal with her shit.

"I'm not trying to 'ruin your high,'" Rachel said, taking Ian's empty seat. "I just don't want you getting your hopes up over nothing."

"Why do people say that?" Ian asked. "I mean, is there a way to keep hope *low*? Isn't the point to have *high* hopes?"

Rachel smiled. "Yeah, I guess maybe. But still, try not to read too much into this. You shared a kiss. And a kiss doesn't mean you'll be getting back together."

"Whose side are you on, here?" Ian leaned against the counter and chugged his water.

"Yours, of course. I'll always be on yours. But I still don't want you to get hurt though. Again."

"Well thanks, really. But I'll be fine. I'm a big boy. And you can roll your damn eyes all you want. You weren't there. You didn't get to feel what I did behind our kiss. Even if he didn't kiss back, I still—"

"Wait." Rachel threw a hand up this time. "He didn't kiss you back? You just said Sam kissed you. What...?" She just sat there, wide-eyed.

Ian brushed her judgment off. "Doesn't matter," he said. Rachel shook her head. "Look, I know I sound crazy.

And who the fuck knows, maybe I am. But Sam still loves me, Rach. *He does.*"

Before Rachel could protest further, the doorbell rang. Ian, riding the high just thinking of Sam brought, stepped out to go answer the door. His heart sped up at the thought of Sam being on the other side, ready to apologize for turning him away last night, ready to take Ian back. Seeing Sam there would damn sure make an already better-than-average morning almost perfect.

But Sam wasn't the one ringing the doorbell. Not even fucking close.

Shit.

"Uh, what the hell are you doing here?" The face on the other side of his door took Ian by surprise. His entire body tensed up, ready to strike if need be.

"You got a minute?" Noah asked. The cheesy ass nice-guy bit he had been peddling since Ian first laid eyes on him had disappeared. The dude standing on his sister's front porch was six kinds of pissed.

And Ian had three guesses about what.

"Listen," Ian said, "about last night—" He didn't get the chance to finish what he wanted to say, how he didn't regret or feel sorry about what went down with Sam, because Noah's fist introduced itself to his face and Ian flew into the wall behind him. A tiny table with a vase of fake flowers became a casualty, splintering under Ian's crushing weight. "Jesus Christ!" Ian grabbed his nose. Tasted blood. Wanted to *kill* the mother fucker.

But he didn't. Son of a bitch, did he want to. But he understood. He got where Noah came from. Hell, he knew he would have done the same thing if he had been Noah. So, he took the punch and kept his mouth shut even though it hurt worse to keep quiet than to deal with what would no doubt be a broken nose. He almost laughed, because all this time he had thought Noah would be the one on the floor bleeding from his fucking face.

"What the hell!" Rachel came from out of nowhere. She eyed Noah and Ian both, unsure what to do until she saw the blood. She rushed to Ian. "Jesus, are you okay?" She pawed at his face, trying to see the damage.

"Do I fucking look okay?" Ian pushed her hands away because even having them close hurt. His entire face throbbed like a son of a bitch and had already started to plump up. Blood drenched his hand and ran down his arm. Rachel leapt up and disappeared, coming back with a hand towel and pressing the fabric hard against his nose. "Ow! Fuck!" He yelped and squirmed and snatched the towel from her hand. "Jesus, man, just stop. I'll do it myself."

"Stay the hell away from Sam." Noah's voice grabbed Rachel and Ian's attention and they both stared at him. "You fucking hear me?"

Rachel charged at him. Pushed him out onto the porch. "Leave. *Now*," she said, closing the door. Noah threw up an arm to stop her.

"We're getting married," he said. "So, stay the hell out of our lives."

"Go!" Rachel shoved the door with all her might and it slammed shut. She took a few deep breaths and spun to face her brother, bloody and crumpled on the floor.

Ian's entire world, the life he had already destroyed and the one he desperately wanted to rebuild, incinerated with Noah's words. Like an atom bomb had been set off in his head, obliterating everything.

We're getting married.

This was it. The spark igniting between them was over. All over. His plan to win Sam back. Love him again. Be happy again. Those three little words killed everything.

"God, Ian, I'm so sorry." Rachel appeared at his side, helping him up off the floor. When had he sat down? Did Noah knock him on his ass? Or did what he said?

"You... You knew." Ian didn't have to ask. He knew the truth. He knew now what Rachel had been keeping from him, not telling him all this time. He sensed something the second he first mentioned Sam's name, mentioned going to see him. There had been something off with her, even though they had been getting along better than they had in years. He never brought up the uneasy feeling he'd had because he assumed whatever she kept hidden had to be something personal she didn't want to talk about. But the secret she'd been keeping wasn't about her. No. His sister fucking *knew*.

"I couldn't tell you," Rachel finally confessed. "I wanted to. God, Ian, I wanted to tell you so you would forget about trying to win him back. I just—"

"Couldn't hurt me," Ian interjected. "Seems to be what you're good at." He pulled the towel from his nose and stared down at the bright red streaks in the white fabric. Almost the entire thing had soaked through, so he stuck a finger above his lip. Bleeding seemed under control.

"You're my brother, Ian. I love you. I don't ever want to hurt you."

Ian stopped just as they made their way to the bathroom down the hall and turned to face her. "Too fucking late," he said before closing the door behind him, locking Rachel and the world out.

Chapter Seventeen

Ian spent the next few days not giving a shit about anything. He didn't care about eating or showering or going to see his asshole PO. He had lost Sam all over again. For good this time. He had played his last hand. Taken his last chance. Game over. Everything else seemed pointless in his mind. Yeah, somewhere in his head he knew how fucked up it was to think your life meant nothing because some guy dumped you or wouldn't take you back, but things were different for him. What he felt wasn't something he could explain, not that his personal life needed explaining to anybody even if he could. His feelings for Sam, what they once meant to each other—their connection went far beyond a childhood crush or some stupid teenage angst-driven puppy love. Their bond was real. Forever. At least he had thought so.

Now, everything felt different. Everything had changed, warped, no longer fit into the right space anymore. Which explained why Ian couldn't see the point in worrying about shit like food or pissing in a damn cup. None of the trivial junk in life mattered without Sam. Nothing mattered but the one thing he had always been sure of. The one thing which never disappointed him, never let him down. He had just twisted the top off his first beer of the day when a knock on the door stopped him and Rachel busted in.

"Shit," he said, sloshing beer on his chest. Foam rolled off his sides and soaked the sheets. "Damn, Rach, what's the fucking point of knocking? What if I'd been jacking off or something?"

"Please," Rachel said, stopping at the foot of his bed. "You've been doing that since you were thirteen. I'm surely not gonna freak out now."

Ian rolled his eyes and set his beer on the nightstand. "What the hell do you want?" Rachel didn't say a word. Just walked over and snatched the bottle away from him. "What the fuck?"

"When's the last time you drank?" Rachel stood beside his bed, bottle in hand, waiting. Ian's eyes were locked on the beer he had been so fucking ready to funnel.

"None of your damn business," he snapped. "Now give me back my fucking beer." She ignored his begging and walked back across the floor to his bedroom door. "I'm serious, Rachel. Leave me the fuck alone."

She spun around. "I'm serious, too, Ian. You have to see your PO today."

Ian flopped against the headboard. "Fuck no."

Rachel ignored him. "You need to get out of bed, take a shower because you stink, and go get one of those kit thingies to flush the alcohol out of your system." She glanced at the clock on the nightstand. "It's almost nine. You have until five." Ian didn't move. Rachel stood there eyeballing him until he grunted and swung his legs to the floor.

"You can be a real bitch when you wanna be." He had his elbows on his knees and his head in his hands. His stomach lurched because all he'd had in the past twenty-four plus hours other than alcohol were a few crackers and a ham sandwich. He closed his eyes to stop the swaying.

"Maybe so," Rachel said, "but you're getting your ass to your probation office today."

Ian stood up. Ran a hand through his hair and took a deep breath. "Jesus, why do you care?" he asked, turning to glare at her. "Seriously. Why? I don't."

"*That's* why," Rachel answered. "You may not care right now but I do. I always do. I know your life sucks really badly and you wish it would all be over so you could just move to some stupid hole in the ground somewhere until you die. I get that. But you're a grown-ass man, Ian. You're not a kid anymore. So stop acting like one."

"Fuck you."

"Whatever. Just stop acting like a spoiled teenager and get a shower."

"All right. Damn, back off." He crossed the room and pulled some underwear and socks from his dresser. Grabbed some jeans and a T-shirt from the open-faced closet in the corner.

"You can walk around with an attitude all you want," Rachel said. "And you can blame me or Sam or—"

"Don't say his fucking name," he interrupted, glaring at her. "After what you did to me, you don't get to use him against me."

"You can blame me or *him* or anybody else you want to for everything wrong in your life, Ian, but the truth is all the shit you're going through is all your fault. You're in trouble right now because of something *you* did. So be a man and face the truth. Deal with your problems until you figure out how to solve them the right way. Then get your shit together and stop acting like the entire world owes you something. No one owes you anything."

Ian practically ignored her and walked past her. "Do me a favor," he said as he headed to the bathroom. "Be somewhere else when I get out."

*

Rachel *was* gone when he came out of the bathroom, dressed and ready to go. Well, not *ready* ready; he wasn't ready to go anywhere because he didn't give a shit about passing his damn piss test. Had half a mind to fail on purpose so he could get the hell away from Rachel and Sam for a while. Take a break.

The other half is the reason he left the house for the first time since Noah had broken his nose and his life. The reason he got the stupid cleanse kit and came back to Rachel's to drink the nasty fucking liquid and about ten gallons of water before heading to his probation officer for yet another mandated invasion of his privacy. His nerves amped up for this test, though, because this would be the closest he had come to the cutoff time for drinking and still pissing clean. Or clean enough to fool the simpleminded fucks who tested pee for a living. He would never tell Rachel, but he'd already googled the exact amount of time he needed to flush his system. Yeah, he didn't give a shit, for the most part, but the tiniest, fractured piece of him held out hope he would win Sam back one day, so he couldn't *actually* give up. Not yet.

Which is why the second he got out of his PO's office with an all-clear he headed to Final Draft. He planned on drowning the hopeful part of himself for good.

*

He stepped into the bar just as the blue-collar crowd poured in. Almost five-thirty and the place had gotten so close to packed, he had to stand around and wait to grab a barstool. He took the first open seat at the bar and watched Stacey running like a chicken with her head cut off, trying to fill all the orders pouring in. Construction workers, some after-shift cops, a couple city employees; the place held a mix of everything his tiny suburb of Chicago had to offer. The cogs in the wheel to keep the city spinning. He saw beer after beer, shot after shot cross the bar, sitting in silence waiting his turn. Stacey caught sight of him after what felt like forever. She smiled and headed his way.

"Damn, I'm actually glad to see you," she said. "This place is insane tonight. We haven't been this busy since Christmas." She already had a mug filled for him, the froth floating on top making his mouth water. "Where the hell you been?"

Ian downed a third of the glass, the ice-cold brew settling his queasy stomach like nothing else could. "Been laying low," he said after letting a large belch bellow across the bar. "I've had a shitty week."

Stacey gestured to the room. "Remember the club I told you about?"

Ian laughed. "Yeah, yeah. Another?"

She smiled. "You bet." She disappeared, rushing back with another two full mugs before waving adios and heading out to thin the herd. As busy as the bar had become, he didn't see much of her for a while, other than the second or two she could spare to slide a beer down to him. He sat there happy as a clam by himself getting shitfaced while the room buzzed around him. The din rose as the crowd grew thick as weeds. By the time the bar reached near capacity—which probably wasn't even a hundred bodies, given the entire floor plan couldn't have been bigger than a studio apartment—Ian had to be about six sheets to the wind. He fished his wallet from his back pocket and tossed a few twenties on the bar. He gave the polished oak a knock and waved and pointed to the money when Stacey finally acknowledged him. She waved back and he left.

The air outside felt good. He had gotten overheated as the beer started hitting him, so a frigid wind blasting his face was just what he needed. He sucked in a few deep breaths before making his way down the sidewalk. The noise pouring out of Final Draft, and the far less busy O'Neill's three stops down, began to wane as he turned a corner to a quieter, darker side street. He hugged the buildings until they opened up to a massive, empty lot, save for one beat-up old Ford sitting almost dead center. A shortcut Stacey had told him about one night after he complained about having to walk every fucking where he went. He didn't shave much time off his trip, but the lot did avoid the two streets in the area the late-night cops loved to ride up and down searching for partiers who'd had too much to drink, so he said a silent thank-you Stacey had clued him in. Ian glanced at the truck but paid no mind as he headed to the northeast corner of the lot.

But he damn sure should have. His night might have turned out a lot different if he had.

Chapter Eighteen

Ian had been on plenty of drug-induced trips before. He had flown through the neon-colored clouds. He'd walked across a crystal-clear ocean while the bug-eyed whales and sharks below stared up at him and smiled. He'd even flown like a featherless, purple eagle over mountains of tie-dyed swirls. He could get lost in a haze like a fucking pro.

But the magic carpet ride he currently rode on felt different. There were no bright clouds. No smiling sea creatures. He wasn't flying—the complete opposite, in fact. He felt like he had been strapped down, weighted, gravity times a million. His body had never felt so heavy, so immobile. And Jesus, the cold. A painful fucking cold. Yet, he didn't really *feel* cold. He was just...there. There in the darkness and cold, like nothing.

He wanted to wake up. Had been trying to for an eternity. But something held him back. Drugs? Too much whiskey? He didn't know, but for some reason he couldn't make his body do what he wanted. Inside, he felt like a fucking warrior on the battlefield, swinging his sword, slicing in half everyone and everything in his way. On the outside though? Nothing.

"He seems good today."

Words split the darkness. Ian could see them cutting through, tiny pinholes of light where they entered. They floated down to him from a million miles away, transparent and wobbly, but there. They landed on his chest. Vibrated in time with his heartbeat. He wanted to touch them. Feel them. Remember them. Couldn't.

"He does. So much better."

More words came down out of the dark. More specks of light. These felt closer, though, like the emptiness around him had shrunk by half. They landed just like the ones before, but beside him this time. He could feel them burrowing beneath him, finding a nice warm spot to live.

"Can he hear me?"

"Yes!" Ian screamed his answer as loud as he could. No sound came. His lips wouldn't open. His voice wouldn't work. His mind kept shouting the word over and over, desperate to be heard, but his body refused. He watched the words slip beneath him like the others. He could feel them there, just under his back. They were pushing him. Pushing him up toward the lighted pinpricks. He pleaded for more words to come, to carry him all the way up so he could see.

"I think he can. Even if he can't, don't stop talking to him. He needs to hear us."

"Are you doing okay?"

"I've been better, but I'm fine considering. I'm just happy he's here."

"Yeah, me too."

Ian rose higher and higher as the words filled the darkness around him. As he inched closer to the light, now so bright he could make out things like curtains and a window, sunlight and trees, his body began to wake up. His arms tingled. His legs. His throat itched like a thousand bees nested there. His eyes were heavy, but they always were when he got drugged out of his mind. His heavy lids didn't matter though. They were opening, letting him see again. Walls. A TV. People.

Sam.

In a split second Ian's brain was bombarded with images and light and sound, like an atom bomb going off in his fucking face. He closed his eyes and winced at the blinding pain, tried to turn away but couldn't. Pain shot out everywhere, all-consuming. His head, face, arms, stomach—every inch of him felt on fire, millions of stings over and over, never ending. He wanted to die.

"Oh, my God." He heard words again, this time only inches from him. They didn't float to him like before, just hung in the air for a moment before dissipating like words always do. Something landed on his hand, soft like a butterfly or a snowflake. Had he gone outside? He couldn't be sure, his brain too warped to distinguish place and time. But this touch felt different from when the words had sat on his bare chest. This *felt* real even if he couldn't be sure. The sensation of the light touch traveled up his arm in a streak of stinging pain, radiating down over him once the pain reached the top of his head. His stomach turned as he moved, like a ship in a hurricane.

"Get a doctor." Ian flinched at the sound. Grunted at the pain. Tried to run away from the hurting but couldn't. All he could do to protest, make the torture stop, was brush a finger against whatever had settled on his hand.

"He touched me. Rachel, he touched me."

Ian recognized the voice. Somewhere in his mind, he knew whose voice he had just heard. He knew the tone, the inflection, so familiar and safe. He didn't know who the sound belonged to, and yet he somehow did. He couldn't explain how knowing and not knowing at the same time could even be possible. It almost felt like the voice had been his own, outside his body, being carried by someone else. He missed the voice the second the sound vanished, wishing like hell the melody would never stop.

"Doctor's coming. This is amazing."

This voice he knew too. This one held a special place for him, just like the one before, but in a different way. He didn't feel like this voice belonged to him though, like the other, but maybe a *part* of him in some weird way. This one sounded different too. More sadness. Or overwhelming joy. Either way, the voice soothed Ian. They both did.

"Ian? Can—Can you hear me, Ian?"

The first voice, the one he never wanted to be without again, hung in his ear. Low, comforting, pleading. Ian wanted nothing more than to grab hold of the words and never let go. He tried to speak back, but his own words were caged inside him, trapped behind layers of excruciating pain. He grunted instead, wishing like hell he could tell the voice, "Don't go."

"I'm not going anywhere. I'm right here." The voice heard him somehow. Did the words come from inside his head? Did *all* of this, the window and trees and walls and pain, exist only in his head? No. Couldn't be. Ian had been in his own head when tripping. This felt different. The pain too real, too present, to be his imagination. And the voices, both had feeling, emotion. They couldn't be faked by a psychedelic.

"Ian?" The higher-pitched voice again. God, why couldn't he fucking remember where he knew the sound from? "Ian, I'm here too. We're both here and we want you to wake up. Can you wake up for us? Can you open your eyes?"

Desperation to give the voices what they wanted, what he himself wanted, overwhelmed him. He tried with everything inside him to open his eyes. He focused every muscle in his body. Blocked out the overwhelming pain as best he could. Hell, he even prayed to a God he wasn't even sure he believed in anymore. He could see his eyelids, clamped down tight like they had been nailed shut. He zeroed in on them, put all his energy into making them listen to the screaming in his head to *Open! Open! Fucking open!*

And they did.

Chapter Nineteen

Ian's entire world erupted the second his eyes opened. The light hit them hard, as if the sun sat directly on his face. His body burned like an inferno, and he rapid-fire blinked over and over trying to make the excruciating pain stop. His body felt how ground beef looked, the pain so intense, like nothing he had ever experienced before. Torture. Crippling fucking torture. He wanted to crawl back into the cold darkness until everything went black again.

But at least he had finally woken up. After what felt like an eternity in the empty hollow of his mind, he was 100 percent awake. Yeah, every single fucking inch of him hurt like he had never hurt before, but he felt grateful to be alive and no longer stuck in some wigged-out phantom zone his head had created. Being alive and able to feel and see and know he wasn't dead felt amazing.

Except for the choking.

The choking started just seconds after he came to. An intense, stabbing pain shot up and down the length of this throat, like someone had strangled him. He tried to reach up and stop whoever had their hands in a death grip around his throat but his stupid arms wouldn't move, wouldn't help save his life. He tried to yell out for help but his vocal chords were being crushed. He grunted in protest and felt a hand, heavier this time, on his.

"Don't struggle, you will only make things worse. They're on their way now." The voice. Rachel's voice. Her voice felt higher pitched in his ears, the one he knew had been a part of him. He made his eyes move toward the sound, slow and painful until her face filled his vision. She smiled ear to ear. Still the same dork as always.

"Hi," she said, and Ian would've smiled like a dork too if he wasn't still choking. The sensation of being drowned with sand had eased up some, but still hurt like a bitch. "God, am I glad to see those beautiful green eyes." Rachel's face seemed fuzzy, a bit distorted, but Ian could see she had been crying. But she smiled too, so she couldn't be sad. He didn't understand the tears on her cheeks. "Guess who's here?" Ian stared hard at her. He watched her eyes leave his and he made his eyes follow.

Sam.

"Hey." Sam's voice. Jesus. The voice he had heard just out of the darkness. The voice that brought him back from wherever he had been, the voice he missed most when it disappeared, made him feel whole again, even though every other part of him splintered. Ian would have given his fucking life to smile right then. Say hi back. Let Sam know he heard him. But he could only stare. Watch Sam's face. Sam smiled too, like Rachel, but even through the blurry haze Ian could tell Sam wasn't as happy as she had been. Sam's face looked somber. Ian had no fucking clue how he even knew the word but there it sat, in his head just waiting to be used. Sam's face, so sad, drawn down even with the smile. Ian's heart hurt worse than his body when he saw sadness on such a beautiful thing.

"We're both here," Rachel said, and Ian managed to roll his eyes back over to her. "And we are both so, so happy to have you back, Ian. Oh good, the doctors are here." Ian turned to where Sam stood, right inside the door, just as a group of people dressed in some weird fucking dark-colored onesies came in and surrounded his bed. He kept his eyes on one, a cute guy with short blond hair and kind eyes, as he brought his hands to Ian's face.

"Okay, Mr. Fisher," the man said, "we're gonna take this tube out now. It's not going to hurt, but I can't really tell you you will enjoy it either." Ian had no fucking clue what his words meant, and he sure as hell couldn't ask the guy to explain. "I need you to give me a great big cough if you can, okay? Ready? One, two, three." Ian tried to cough but couldn't, the pain shooting up his throat stealing his ability to do any damn thing. So, turns out the cute guy with the kind eyes wasn't so kind after all, because Ian felt pretty sure he'd just ripped Ian's throat right out of his fucking neck. Ian wanted to scream at the guy, punch him. His body still wasn't doing what he wanted, so he settled for grunting and squeezing his eyes shut instead.

"Sorry, sorry," the man said. "But we're done. You did great." Ian opened his eyes like they were glued shut, they felt so damn heavy, and glared at him. He smiled down at Ian like an angel. Angel of Death, given how bad the shit had hurt. At least Ian had stopped choking, so maybe he wasn't such a bad guy after all.

"Wh—" The sound came out before Ian even knew what had happened. He stopped quick though when his vocal chords came to life and tried to rip themselves out of his throat. Shit, the pain went way past intense. He swallowed, which hurt like hell too, over and over, trying to shove his voice box back in place.

"Whoa, there," the guy said. "Don't try to talk just yet, okay? We gotta get you something for your throat. Feels like razor blades in there, huh?" More like a meat grinder, but razor blades were a close second. Ian blinked and the man nodded. "Yeah, you're gonna feel rough for a while, but each day will get easier and easier. I'll have a nurse bring you in something to help." He nodded to someone on the other side of the bed—too exhausted to try to see who—and turned back to Rachel.

"Keep him from trying to say anything if you can," the man said. "He was intubated for quite a while, so talking will only do more damage."

Ian watched Rachel nod. Wipe tears away. "Is he going to be okay now?" she asked. "Since he's awake?"

The man Ian assumed had to be a doctor took a seat on the windowsill behind him and clasped his hands over his crotch. "He will be, eventually. But he has a lot of healing to do. Thankfully there is no indication of anything other than some serious superficial injuries. No internal damage other than the bleeding we've already stopped. His head injuries don't appear to have caused any permanent damage, though we won't know for sure until he's able to speak and we can do a complete evaluation. But from what I can tell, he should be back to normal with a little time."

Ian wondered who the hell this guy was talking about? And why to his sister? Then he remembered all the pain. How he had tried to wake himself up but couldn't. How his arms wouldn't move and his voice didn't seem to work. All the nurses and tubes and talk of head wounds and permanent damage...

He was the patient.

They were talking about *him*.

Chapter Twenty

Ian grunted. Since he couldn't use his fucking words to tell mister asshat doctor where to shove his prognosis, he opted instead for frustrated growls and some serious eye blinking. Damn, even blinking hurt like a son of a bitch, and the beeping coming from behind him sped up. But he would suffer through the pain if the guy would just shut up. The doctor and Rachel both stepped up to his bed. Anger rose inside Ian, and he wanted to punch them both for sitting there talking about him like some kind of goddamned cripple. He could barely stand the sight of them, too disgusted with the shit they were saying.

Sam stood there, on the other side of his bed. The nice side, where no one said he was broken, Sam stood watch. His protector. The one person Ian knew he could count on to be there when others turned on him. He pushed through the pain and attempted a smile.

Sam smiled back, a bit more genuinely this time. "Hey," he said, the only word he had spoken since Ian opened his eyes, but somehow a simple "hey" had been just right. The word had set Ian at ease, let him know as long as Sam lingered next to him, the junk Rachel and the doctor were spewing didn't matter. His pain didn't matter. Nothing did. Just Sam.

His heartbeat slowed. The crazy-fast beeping went back to a normal distraction. Even the pain seemed to let up a bit, though not enough to make a huge difference in how he felt. Ian kept his eyes locked on Sam. Wanted to say something to him so bad he opened his mouth. His throat burned and stung, but no sound came out.

"I'm kind of enjoying you not being able to talk," Sam said, his smile wide and warm and hitting Ian just the right way. "You've always loved hearing the sound of your own voice." Sam laughed and it was the best fucking thing Ian had ever heard. He watched Sam watching him. Felt his hand on his arm, his fingers caressing the skin there. His touch hurt, but even if Ian could talk, he wouldn't tell him to stop. He would deal with the pain for the rest of his damn life if he could feel Sam's skin against his.

His memories were a little screwed up, hazy and out of focus and he couldn't be sure of the order they were in, but he remembered his life with Sam. How perfect things were, back when they first met and fell in love and were ready to spend every second together. Then came the images of a funeral, two caskets, unbearable pain, leaving. He left Sam. Screwed up the life he had always wanted. Then came back like he had done nothing wrong. Tried to pick up where he and Sam had left off. He had been such an asshole to Sam, and to his boyfriend. Ian struggled to remember the guy's name until words flooded his mind. A headline. A photo. A wedding.

Noah. And *he* had Sam now, not Ian. And they were getting married.

Ian's heart hurt so bad he thought his chest would explode. The annoying fucking beeping skyrocketed. More bells and whistles joined in. His head split open, his body shook with the pain of remembering. He closed his eyes to forget. He just wanted to forget.

*

When he woke up again, a much simpler process this time, Ian's was alone in his room. He blinked several times to try to bring his surroundings into focus. He got a somewhat blurred version at best and gave up. He could hear voices, just outside the open door, but couldn't make out the words. Something about setbacks and stress and triggers and he stopped straining to make out more. Straining hurt too fucking much. Everything hurt too fucking much. Had he been in an accident, like his parents? Did he finally cross the line he had been toeing for almost a year and try to off himself? He was pissed off not being able to remember what the hell had happened to him. Every nasty thing he ever did to Sam he could call up on demand; how he ended up like a slab of tenderized steak in a fucking hospital bed...nothing. Between the pain and growing frustration, Ian felt worse than shit.

The wall over his head made a series of sounds he had never heard before and the hot doc and his sister walked back into the room. He watched the doctor as he went to said machine and punched some buttons to make the noises stop. He smiled when he made eye contact with Ian.

"Feeling better?" he asked. Ian nodded, frustrated even more because he couldn't say the fucking word "yes." "Wonderful. Now Ian—your sister said I should call you Ian. Cool?" Ian nodded again. Doc smiled. "Cool. What I need from you, Ian, is to try to not get too worked up or mad at yourself for not being able to do all the things I know you're wanting to do right now, okay?" Shit, somehow the man had crawled into Ian's head. "If you can be a little patient, I promise you're gonna feel so much better. And trust me, you'll be talking up a storm in no time. You'll be up walking around again, showing off your pretty face to all the nurses. Just bear with us while we take care of you. Can you do all that for me, Ian?" Ian didn't want to. He wanted out of his fucking hospital bed *yesterday*, but he didn't have much of a choice. He nodded. "Great. I'll be back in to check on you soon." He left the room and Ian followed him with his eyes until he saw Rachel smiling at him.

"Hey there," she said, stepping up to the bed. "I know you would've rolled your eyes at him if you could have, but you need to do what he says, okay?" Ian squinted and Rachel laughed. "What's that, your temporary version of the middle finger?" He cleared his throat and blinked.

"I know you're aggravated right now, Ian. And mad and frustrated and ready to get the hell out of here. But..." Rachel turned away, stared out the window for a few seconds before turning back so he could see her face. She smiled again, a tight-lipped one she used when she didn't feel on the inside how she knew people wanted her to appear on the outside. Ian added worry to his list of emotions. He could see how fucking sad this all made her, and how hard she tried not to let him see. Her trying to protect him, always, hurt him almost as much as the pain he suffered. "I don't want you to worry about anything," Rachel went on. "You hear me? I've talked to your probation officer, and he's gonna talk to the judge about suspending the rest of your sentence. He seemed genuinely concerned about you, so maybe he can get you out early given...what you've been through."

Ian grunted. Stared wide-eyed at his sister, begging her to tell him what the fuck had happened to him. He saw her struggle, fighting with herself over telling him.

"You don't need to worry about anything right now," she said. Ian's frustration grew, rose up his throat like a geyser. His body clenched up, and through the intense pain he somehow managed to eke out two breathy, almost inaudible words.

"Tell me."

Chapter Twenty-One

As Rachel sat on the edge of his bed explaining to him what had landed him in the hospital in so much pain, Ian struggled to process everything he heard. The words she said, hate crime, press charges, attempted murder, didn't make sense. Not about him. There wasn't a chance in hell he had been the victim of some fucking hate crime. No way. He wouldn't let some asshole get the jump on him. Beat him almost to death. And sure as shit not because he liked guys. But Rachel wouldn't make up such a lie. Not something like this. Even if he had tried to kill himself, she wouldn't try to convince him someone had tried to kill him because of who he fucking slept with.

Memories instantly flooded Ian's mind, one after the other, like an ocean. He didn't need to listen to Rachel anymore. He began reliving in his head exactly what had happened.

He'd gotten drunk at Final Draft. Decided to take Stacey's shortcut on his way home to avoid cops. There had been...*something* in the empty parking lot. He couldn't make out what exactly, the images way too distorted to form a clear picture. But he could remember seeing a shape. An object. He remembered noticing but not giving a second thought. Just kept walking. He had been upset over the news Sam would be marrying Noah and wanted to drink until he didn't hurt anymore. By the time he headed toward home, he had succeeded. His had gotten his mind so out of whack he didn't see the attack coming. He sure as shit felt every second though.

The first blow across the back of his head had been beyond intense. Ian couldn't think of a word to describe the feeling well enough, but bad would do. The worst pain he had ever felt in his life. He fell forward. Tried to stop himself with his hands. The bones in one of his wrists popped when they broke. Another blow to his head, just above the neck, and everything had gone dark. He could still hear and feel every excruciating hit though. The cracking noises his ribs made as heavy boots kicked at them like a soccer ball. The sound of—metal? wood?—against his legs, arms, back. A booted foot found his face, connected with the bones behind his skin. Blood pooled in his mouth and his eye socket exploded. He remembered crying out for his attacker to stop but he could barely get the sound out from all the blood, a wet, mangled gurgling where the words should have been.

Ian also remembered voices. He couldn't recall how many, or whether they were male or female, but he did remember more than one. His brain hurt too much to try to piece together complete sentences, but phrases like "fucking faggot" and "wanna kill all the fucking queers" stuck out in his head. Rachel hadn't lied or made up a story to cover the truth. He *had* been beaten up. Because he was gay.

"Hey, hey, don't, Ian." Rachel's voice pulled him out of the horrible memories and Ian looked at her. Her face blurred and distorted in his vision and he could barely make out her features. She brought a hand to his face, something gripped tight in her fingers, and touched his cheek. "Don't cry," she said. "If you let this beat you, Ian, then they win." She did her best to sound positive, even smiled when she spoke, but Ian saw through the bullshit, even in his drugged state. He could see her fear, feel her broken heart. Which pissed him off even more.

He tried to sit up. Tried to lift his arms, bend his knees, turn over on his fucking side. Anything to get out of the damn bed and find the pricks who thought they could get away with using him as a fucking punching bag. Rachel gave his arm a gentle squeeze and he didn't even wince at the pain her touch caused.

"Stop," she said, her voice soft and comforting. "This is why I didn't want to tell you. I knew you would be upset and getting mad wouldn't be good for you right now. I know you want to find whoever did this and make them pay, but you can't. You hear me, Ian? Don't think about any of what happened right now. You *have* to focus on getting well. You have a long road ahead of you."

Ian mustered the strength to whisper, "How long?"

"They aren't sure," Rachel answered. "Dr. Hill said it would take some time but—" Ian grunted, and Rachel stopped talking. "What?" she asked.

Ian forced out the word, "here."

Rachel sat confused for a second before she realized what he had tried to say. "Oh." Her smile faded and she pulled her gaze away for a second. "Ian," she finally said. "Knowing how long you've been here isn't going to change anything. Knowing won't help you get better. Just focus on getting out. Getting back home." Ian grunted again. Focused his energy into his hand still beneath hers. He managed to lift his fingers and lace them with hers. When she looked back up at him, tears streaked her face. "You've been here eleven days."

Eleven days.

Jesus.

Some assholes jumped Ian and put him in the hospital, and he had been there for eleven fucking days and couldn't remember a single one of them. His entire body throbbed from the pain, his brain near mush, and his voice all but gone. All because somebody didn't like him because of who the fuck he slept with.

Anger flooded him. Drowned out the pain and the worry and the fear. Rage poured into all the cuts and bruises and broken bones littering his body, filled in the empty spaces of his mind. His fury consumed him as he lay helpless in a hospital bed, unable to stop the dam holding back his emotions from breaking. But he wouldn't have even if he could. He *wanted* his anger to take over, devour him. Because the second he could, he planned to find the fucks who had jumped him and show them just how gay he was.

"Don't think about it, Ian. Dwelling on a number won't help." Rachel still sat next to him, holding his hand. He stared hard at her, saw the worry and concern she had for him. As much as he wanted to kill the people who had hurt him, he knew he couldn't. He couldn't because doing so would hurt *her*. And he never wanted to hurt her again. He had hurt her enough to last ten lifetimes. He wouldn't let himself cause her pain ever again.

He had hurt Sam too. And remembering fucking killed Ian. He wished his beating would have taken those memories away forever so he wouldn't have to face what a piece of shit he was. How cruel he had been to the man he claimed to love. If he could've taken back everything he had done…

"Sam." With each word, each syllable, Ian's voice grew stronger. The progress moved slower than a snail's pace, but he'd take what he could get. The sooner he got his voice back, the sooner he could find Sam and tell him how sorry he felt. And how much he still loved him. Yeah, he had told him already, about a dozen fucking times, but now, after what had happened... He didn't want to miss the chance to say everything he felt.

"He left," Rachel said. "He said he had to get to work, but would stop by to see you tomorrow if he can."

If he can.

Ian knew what Sam meant: If he could get the hell away from Noah again. Those were other memories left unharmed. He remembered how big of a dick Noah had been. And how much Sam didn't love him. Engaged or not, Ian just knew Sam had to still be in love with him. He just hoped he could convince him to call off the wedding while stuck in the damn hospital with no voice.

Chapter Twenty-Two

Sam didn't show up at the hospital the next day to see Ian. Or the day after. For over a week Ian sat in his bed waiting for Sam to show up but he never did. Ian got a little better each day, regained the use of his arms and legs, and even started putting sentences together. He didn't give a shit about any of his progress though. Not fully. Because he wanted Sam. Wanted to see him and talk to him and know if Sam had given up on him yet. On them.

"Your physical therapy starts today. You ready?" Rachel was there—had been every single day since he woke up—and Ian had been so grateful. He had asked her a few days ago about her job and whether she still had one seeing as how she'd missed close to a month already, but she blew him off saying her job would be fine. He figured she had lied so he wouldn't stress out and was probably as unemployed as him, but he didn't push the issue. He knew if she had been lying, she did so for him, whether he wanted her to or not.

"As I'll ever be." His voice barely reached a whisper now, still raspy and weak, like the words had to travel from his gut to get out. The sound reminded Ian of an old man who hung out at Final Draft almost every day a few years back. Ian never knew the guy's name, but he loved to sit at the end of the bar and relive his days in the war and his three marriages, which all ended in divorce. Ian sounded like the man now, all throaty and garbled, and he smiled at the memory. He missed hanging out at the bar. Missed the old guy too. Missed living his damn life.

"Well, just remember not to overdo things, okay? Dr. Hill said you can do more damage than good if you push yourself too far too fast."

"Sc—screw him." Rachel cut her eyes at him and Ian smiled.

"Don't sleep with your doctor, little brother. You'll cause a whole new world of problems, trust me." Ian eyed her this time, but she just gave him a wink and went back to unpacking some of his clothes from an old suitcase their dad had owned.

The nurses had moved him to a private room a few days ago since he would no doubt be living there for the next several weeks. The extra space and privacy were nice, and the dresser and couch and coffee table made him feel less like being trapped in a hospital and more like he had holed-up in a shitty one-room apartment. He didn't care either way to be honest because he wanted to be home. They could have set him up at the fucking Hilton and he wouldn't have been happy. Home. Sam. Life. Those were the only things he wanted.

"I have to go by work and check on a couple things while you're in PT," Rachel said, finishing with his clothes and stowing the suitcase in the tiny closet built into the wall. "But I'll be back before you finish."

Ian shook his head. "Don't," he said. "Fine here alone."

Rachel smiled. "It's so cute how you think you can tell me what to do. *I'm* the older one, remember? Not you, even though you've always thought you were. And I'm the one who can walk so I'll do whatever I want." Ian grunted and got his middle finger halfway up. "Oh good, you're getting your mobility back. Pretty soon you'll be flipping me off just like old times."

Ian huffed and licked his dry lips. "Fuck...you, Rach." She ignored him as she crossed the room and filled a pink plastic cup with water from a pink plastic pitcher sitting on a rolling table thing. Ian eyed the cup in her hand as she moved, the straw sticking straight out at him. He sucked the cup dry the second the straw touched his lips, the cold water like numbing cream to his throat. She set the cup on the table when he finished and peeked at her watch.

"I have to go," she said, scooping up her purse from the chair in the corner and hooking the strap on her shoulder. "Remember, take things easy today. This is your first session. Don't go in there expecting to run a marathon."

Ian nodded. "I won't." He rested his head on his pillows and stared up at the ceiling in frustration. He wasn't expecting a marathon per se, but he would at least like to walk to the fucking bathroom and take a piss without needing a nurse. Being stuck in his bed, stuck in his room, drove him crazy. He needed to get up, move around, go outside, meet people. He had never been social, unless you counted the regulars at Final Draft who knew him by face but couldn't tell you his name if you paid them, but he'd learn to be if becoming a social butterfly meant getting out of there.

"I'm serious," Rachel said, holding the door to his room open. "Stay positive. It's gonna take a while, but you'll get there. Love you." She waved and left the room just as a nurse Ian could tolerate more than the others but couldn't remember her name swooped in.

"How you feeling today?" she said, stopping just short of his bed.

Ian raised an arm and shook his hand back and forth.

The nurse smiled. "Hey, so-so is better. And 'better' is always a good thing." She held an envelope up in front of her. "Guess who got mail?" She shook the white rectangle at him and smiled before handing him the letter. "Want me to open it for you?"

Ian shook his head and took the envelope from her. "I can," he said, and she smiled and left the room. His hands didn't work the way they should just yet, so he took a few minutes to tear through the strip on the back and pry the envelope open. He sat there a second to catch his breath before pulling out the single folded sheet inside.

A letter.

From Sam.

Ian's heart rate shot up, the stupid beeping machine behind him letting everybody know by matching his racing rhythm. He took a few deep, calming breaths and unfolded the letter.

> *Ian,*
>
> *I've heard you're doing a lot better and I'm so happy for you. I know you'll be getting out of there very soon.*
>
> *I'm sorry I haven't been back to see you. Being there, seeing you there...has just been too hard. I know how ridiculous I sound, to say it's hard for me when you're the one stuck in there, in so much pain. But it's the truth. I was there almost every*

day before you woke up. I would sit there with you while Rachel went to eat or take a shower. It was nice. But being there all the time also became too much.

This is so hard to explain, but...I knew I couldn't come back there. I couldn't see you like that again. Seeing you the night the ambulance brought you in, bloody and bruised, your face swollen so much you weren't you. The pain almost killed me, Ian. It broke my heart, because for so long my heart belonged to you. And I think in some ways, it still does. Which is why I have to stay away.

I know saying something like this in a letter isn't fair to you, but I had to let you know I didn't stop coming to see you because I don't care. I stopped because I do. More than I even realized until all this happened. I do care, and I can't. I'm engaged. I'm getting married. I have to not love you anymore. I have to go.

I hope you go home soon. And I hope you have a wonderful life. And who knows, maybe one day you and I will be able to move past the relationship we had and build a new one. As friends.

I know I would love that.

Love,

Sam

Ian crumpled the letter. Ignored the pain in his hand as he flung the paper ball across the room. The life he had been trying to get back since the day he came home began to slip away from him and he didn't know how to hold on. Sam wasn't coming back to see him. He would get married, move on, even though he still loved Ian.

He stopped fighting the tears and let them fall.

Chapter Twenty-Three

Ian cried until the nurses came to take him to physical therapy. He had forgotten all about having to rehabilitate himself, forgotten about the attack after reading Sam's letter. Neither much mattered to be honest. He didn't care anymore. Didn't care about crying in front of the nurses or going to therapy or even getting out of the hospital. He just didn't fucking care. He wanted to stay in bed, stare at the ceiling, do nothing.

But he knew he couldn't. So, he went through the painful process of climbing out of bed and into the wheelchair they had brought for him. Even the tiniest movement brought on excruciating pain, but a welcome distraction from the shit he'd just endured. Sam's good-bye letter hurt almost as much as the beating Ian had taken. More if you were only talking about his heart which was obliterated now, shattered into so many pieces he would never be whole again. Sam's words stole pieces of his heart forever. Those pieces would never come back. The physical pain he had to live through now took away a fraction of the shit-storm though, so Ian faced the challenge like a champ.

*

The physical therapy facility a few floors up from Ian's room was pretty impressive. The department took up an entire level of the hospital, had its own bathrooms, showers, offices, even a small cafeteria serving coffee and sandwiches and bags of gourmet potato chips. Ian had never stepped foot in one before, but he would bet money this therapy center beat out most of the rest.

Elaine had been assigned to wheel him to the torture chamber disguised as a Therapy Center, according to the sign by the double doors. She wore her gray hair loose, with a pair of those old lady glasses hanging on strings so they wouldn't get lost. She always seemed happy. Always. She drove Ian fucking insane sometimes with how cheerful she could be. No way somebody could be in a good mood twenty-four-seven. He sure as hell wasn't. For the last several weeks, his good moods were few and far between.

"Okay, son, here we are." Elaine always called him "son." The word made him uncomfortable at first, given his affinity for all things emotionless, but after a few visits, he started to kind of like hearing "son" instead of Ian. He imagined she said something similar to all her patients, but he hadn't been called son in a long time, so he pretended she just liked him more.

Elaine pressed the tiny rubber pads on the wheels of his chair so he couldn't roll away and came around to face him. A large male nurse Ian had never seen before stood beside her, a standard-issue hospital smile on his face. "You ready?" Elaine asked with an *actual* smile.

Ian cleared his throat, which felt as dry as the fucking Sahara after all the crying. "Ready." Elaine and the other nurse helped him stand. Held him steady a minute until he adjusted to the pain shooting down his legs. Each time he stood up, the throbbing pulses up and down his legs were less and less noticeable so he knew getting up off his ass and moving around helped, but the decreased pain didn't make him hate standing and walking any less though. They took their time getting him over to a bar attached to the wall and let him get a good grip before stepping back.

"This here's Andrew." Elaine gave the big guy a pat on the back. "He'll be helping during your therapy. He's a great guy. Very sweet and patient. You two are gonna get along just fine." She came back up to Ian and put a hand on his shoulder. "Now if you need anything, you just ask Andrew here, and he'll make sure you're taken care of." She leaned in close so only Ian could hear and said, "And if he can't help you, you have him call me." She smiled and left the room, and Ian wanted to go with her. Not because he liked her so much, but because his legs were already starting to ache, and he didn't see Andrew as the understanding type.

"Okay, like Elaine said, I'm Andrew, and I'll be your physical therapy guide." Andrew walked over and took Ian by the arm. "We're gonna try and move along this wall, okay?" He applied some pressure until Ian started walking forward, one hand death-gripping the railing. "I'll be here with you most days," Andrew continued, "but there are other therapists here who will also be helping out."

"Therapist?" Ian asked, his breath coming in short bursts as he walked. "Like a shrink?"

Andrew gave a little laugh. "No, not like a shrink. Although some of us like to think we are. Here, let's have a seat. Take a little break." He gestured to a padded ottoman just to their right and guided Ian over. Once he managed to find a comfortable position, Andrew squatted in front of him. "My job is to get you back to where you were before your injury. Sometimes I'm able to, sometimes not. I won't lie and tell you this will be easy because it won't, but I can promise you I, and every other therapist in this department will work with you any way we can to make sure you leave here as close to a hundred percent, like you were before you came in. Sound good?"

Andrew's words didn't sound good or bad because Ian didn't care one way or the other. He just wanted this to be over with. "Yeah," he said, figuring a "no" would've meant more sitting around talking. He wanted to get up and get moving so he could go back to his room and sleep the rest of this shitty day away.

"Perfect." Andrew smiled and stood up. Held a hand out toward Ian. "I'm ready if you are." Ian didn't want to but took his hand anyway and nothing happened.

"Help me up," he said, glaring up at Andrew with a what-the-hell expression.

Andrew kept smiling but didn't budge. "I said this would be hard, remember? Now, get a good grip on my hand, and pull yourself up. Don't worry, I won't let you fall."

Ian wanted to tell him to go fuck himself, but he kept quiet and did what Andrew said. He took almost an entire minute of death-gripping Andrew's hand to pull himself up, and sweat ran down his face by the time he got there, but finally he stood upright.

"Great job, Ian," Andrew said. "Now, we're gonna walk back the way we came. I won't be holding you up like before, but I'll be right beside you so don't worry about falling. Now, use the railing, and take as much time as you need."

Which Ian did. The walk down the bar, when Andrew held tight to his arm, had only taken about five minutes.

But all by himself? A hell of a lot longer. But Andrew never pushed him, never got frustrated or upset when Ian would cuss under his breath or stop and close his eyes and take deep breaths to calm the fuck down. Andrew stayed calm, positive, and he got Ian back to his wheelchair in one piece.

"See, not too bad, right?" Andrew asked with a crocodile smile.

Ian wiped sweat from his forehead and smiled. "Nah," he said. "Piece of cake."

At least he hadn't lost his ability to tell a fucking lie.

Chapter Twenty-Four

Ian had somehow gone an entire week without thinking of Sam. Well, without *fixating* on Sam. Andrew and the other physical therapists kept his ass worn out every day, so he pretty much slept when he wasn't walking back and forth across the physical therapy room with them or talking to Rachel. He convinced her not to come by every single day, to get back to her own life. She had fought him like a champ, but he won the battle and she cut back to every *other* day. Still too much in Ian's mind but he would take the win.

The grueling therapy he'd been through had been working too. He could get around on his own a bit now. He took forever to get where he wanted to go, but at least he could take a piss without having to hold on to somebody else. The nurses were like drill sergeants and wouldn't let him go anywhere unless one of them stood at his side, though, so he still felt like a prisoner most of the time. But every day he felt closer and closer to getting the hell out of there. Getting back to Sam.

When he got back to his room after his first round of therapy Ian had picked up Sam's crumpled letter off the floor. Straightened the sheet of paper out as best he could. Kept it. He had only pulled the letter from the nightstand drawer next to his bed twice in the last week, and both times he had cried when he re-read Sam's words. As he sat there waiting for the nurses to take him upstairs again, he fished the letter out again for round number three.

Reading Sam's words, imagining his voice in his head, the emotions he must've had when writing those words, Ian couldn't help but cry. He cried because he hurt thinking about Sam agonizing over saying a good-bye Ian knew he didn't want to say. Ian knew Sam still loved him but had to stay away from him because of his relationship with that dick Noah. Which was the main reason Ian fought so hard to get out of there. Yeah, he wanted his life back, his freedom. But he wanted more than anything to go to Sam. See him. Try to stop him from getting married, if he hadn't already.

Ian had been checking the local paper every day. Even the paper's online website. Nothing about Sam and Noah since the engagement announcement. Each time, he held his breath, his lungs growing tighter and tighter until he finished scanning all the articles. Only then would he exhale and get on with his day. He even asked Rachel about Sam's upcoming wedding every time she visited, though after the things she had already kept from him about Sam, he didn't think he could trust whatever she would tell him.

His nurse showed up right on time. He felt happy when he remembered her name, Leah. Ian tucked Sam's letter back in the drawer and got out of bed. He didn't need help getting in the wheelchair anymore, sliding in with minimal pain and unlocking the wheels. Leah headed for the elevators.

"I hope Andrew is ready to work today," he said as they headed up. His voice had grown stronger, with just a little rasp still hanging on.

"You ready to get out of here, huh?" Leah asked. She stood behind him in the elevator, but Ian could feel her smiling.

"Hell yeah. Sick of this place." She laughed and Ian smiled. He had become friends with just about everyone he'd met since waking up in the hospital weeks ago, and though he would never fucking admit so out loud, he would actually miss them when he left. Which would be as soon as possible if he had his way.

Leah stopped his chair just inside the doors to the therapy room and Ian got himself up and to the railing against the wall. Andrew appeared in a second.

"Hey, Ian," he said, clapping Ian on the shoulder. "Looks like somebody's ready to go."

"Faster I get better, the faster I get out," Ian said, gripping the bar. "Let's walk."

Andrew stopped him. "We're not walking today, actually," he said. Ian cocked a brow. "Nope. Time for you to build some muscle. Come on." He walked beside Ian like he always did as he led them to the far side of the room where a small gym had been installed. Ian had seen the workout equipment his first day there but never paid the setup much attention. Since his legs had taken most of the beating—they were both shattered, and he went through two different surgeries to get them right again—he just assumed all his time in therapy would be spent learning to walk again.

"For real?" he asked when Andrew started loading up the leg press with weights.

"For real. You're walking like a pro. But still a little wobbly and unsure. Building up a little muscle should help so"—he patted the giant bench—"hop on."

Ian felt over the fucking moon excited for the chance to lift weights. He had grown sick of all the walking and leg exercises and shit about a day after he'd started, so getting to do something he liked was a treat. Plus, he'd walk out of there with some great legs. A win-win.

"I'll be right over here helping another patient," Andrew said after Ian had done a few reps and Andrew seemed confident he could manage without someone on top of him. "I'll be keeping an eye on you, though, so no slacking off." He smiled as he walked away, and Ian focused on pushing the hell out of those weights. He felt the burn all the way up his back, each rep painful but nothing he couldn't handle. He took his time, did things the smart way instead of overexerting himself, something he learned the very first day. Ten reps in and he panted like he'd run a mile. He moved like a snail as he brought his knees to his chest and took a beat.

"Nice job." A voice Ian didn't recognize came up behind him. "Hell, you don't even need therapy."

"Thanks," Ian said, trying to get a glimpse of the guy standing just out of his line of sight. He struggled to sit upright. "You should give it a try. It's pretty cool." The man came into view and Ian wanted to eat his own fucking foot. "Ah, shit man. I'm—sorry. Sorry." He couldn't take his eyes off the man's legs. One tan, well-defined, an athlete's leg. The other—

"Titanium," the guy answered before Ian could take a guess, like he'd hopped inside Ian's head. The guy gave his artificial leg a few raps and smiled. "Pretty cool, huh?"

"Uh...yeah. Cool." Ian didn't know what to say. He wasn't an idiot and didn't live under a fucking rock. He knew there were millions of people with prosthetic limbs. He had just never seen one up close and in person.

"Name's Josh." The guy leaned forward and stuck out his hand.

"Uh, Ian." Ian gave his outstretched hand a firm shake. Josh had an All-American appeal: buzz-cut hair, quarterback face, great smile. His eyes were what drew Ian in though. They were a deep, haunting blue. Just like Sam's.

And just as fast, Sam filled Ian's head again, taking over as he always did. Ian tried to fight off images of Sam, his eyes, his lips, his—he stood no fucking chance winning the battle. He stood up, bounced around a bit to try to shake off all the images. Then he stopped and stared at Josh, wide-eyed with panic.

"Dammit, dude," he said. "Was I being rude, or insensitive or something?"

Josh's brow rose. "What, you jumping around like crazy? Nah, man, just...weird as hell." He laughed and set Ian at ease. "Listen, man," he went on, "no worries, okay? So, I got a fake leg. No big deal. We all got our problems." He gave Ian a once over. "Can't really say I can see yours as easy as you can see mine though."

Ian shook his head. "Nah, my messed up shit is inside. Oh, uh... I'm saying you not having a leg is messed up. Or a *real* leg, I mean. Fuck."

Josh laughed hard. One of those deep belly laughs you have to hunch over to get out. "Oh man, I can tell I'm gonna have fun messing with you." He shook his head and hopped on the weight bench next to Ian's station. He started benching the weights already on the bar, well over a hundred pounds from what Ian could see, stopping after a quick set of ten.

"Wow," Ian said, impressed. "Nice job."

"Ah. Thanks, man." Josh sat up on the bench and Ian noticed his breathing had almost returned to normal. If Ian had lifted so much weight so fast, he would've needed a minute—or ten. "I worked out a lot after. Not much else I could do for a while."

"After?" Ian asked. Josh took a hit off his water bottle and then used the metal container to bang his titanium leg again. Ian nodded, feeling like a moron.

"You can ask if you want," Josh said, hopping up to add more weight to the bar. Ian hadn't thought about asking anything, but the second Josh said he had no problem sharing, he couldn't *not* ask.

"How'd it happen?"

Josh busied himself with switching out the smaller weights for some bigger ones, pushing the total just over two-fifteen. "Afghanistan," he said, returning to the bench.

"No shit?" Ian slid down on the leg press and got comfortable.

"No shit." Josh wiped his brow with a rag he had next to his water bottle, which he scooped up and tossed back. "Did two tours. Would've done more but, well... Those IEDs can be a real bitch."

Ian didn't know what to say. Seeing Josh sitting there, confident and outgoing and badass as shit after having his fucking *leg blown off*, made him feel like an even bigger loser for wallowing in self-pity for getting beat up. Sure, the attack had been bad, hurt like hell, but at least he would be going home with all his limbs. This guy though...

"Wow, man," Ian said, still in shock. "You're pretty fucking amazing."

Josh laughed and shook his head. "Thanks, man, but I'm no different from you or anybody else. I had a job to do, got hurt, now I'm doing something else."

Ian's head shook right back without him even realizing. "No way, man. You are so much better than me. Better than most, I'd say. I mean, you took a fucking *bomb* for us. That's...wow."

Josh slid back on the bench. Got positioned beneath all the weight on the bar. Set his grip. "Proud to do it," he said before lifting the bar and bringing the weight down to his chest. Back up, back down. Over and over, passing the ten leg pushes Ian managed to do. Fifteen, sixteen, seventeen... Ian just sat there watching this fucking real-life Superman do his thing.

He didn't think of Sam the rest of the night.

Chapter Twenty-Five

Ian had never been more excited to go to therapy than the day after meeting Josh. His new outlook had nothing to do with Josh's hotness or insane fucking physical shape, titanium leg and all. His attitude, his personality, and how positive he seemed is what drew Ian in. For months now—hell, over a *year*—Ian had been moping his way through life, hating everything around him, inside him. Then he meets a man who almost fucking died because some crazy wanted to be a hero for his fucked-up cause and everything he had ever thought about himself warped and shifted out of focus. He hadn't felt so alive since he first met Sam.

Sam had the same effect on Ian too. Sam's spirit dominated a space, so booming and in your face, you couldn't help but be drawn to him. Ian saw the same thing in Josh. A super-huge, dominating spirit so infectious you couldn't stop yourself being sucked right into his orbit.

Ian almost jumped out of the wheelchair the second Elaine dropped him off for therapy, shouting thanks over his shoulder before running—his version of running, anyway—to the gym area, where Josh had just settled in.

"Hey, Ian, good to see you, man." Josh had his hand out again by the time Ian got to him and Ian gave the large paw a firm shake. "Legs again today?"

Ian rolled his eyes. "Legs *every* day, man," he answered, and Josh laughed. "Begged Andrew to let me get some upper body work in but he shot me down."

"Yeah, well, not everybody can look this good." Josh gave his chest a double-tap and threw his hands up in the air and flashed a goofy grin. He had Ian laughing so hard his stomach hurt.

"Dude, don't *ever* do that again. For real." He couldn't stop laughing as he climbed onto the leg press machine and nodded over to Andrew, signaling he was ready to go, and started his workout. He would steal glances of Josh as he did, fascinated by how smooth the man moved with only one leg. Yeah, he knew he had *two*, but one wasn't attached to his body. Not in the natural way, anyway. Ian watched Josh navigate as if he had been born half machine.

Ian finished up his reps, another set of ten, Andrew's orders, and took a breather. Josh finished his set of *twenty* in about the same amount of time and sat up.

"So, tell me," Ian said, swinging his legs to the floor and sitting upright. "Why are you doing physical therapy on your arms if your leg is where you got hurt?"

"I had some muscle and ligament damage from the IED," Josh answered, rotating his arm. "Jacked my shoulder up pretty bad. Doc has me doing therapy for a few weeks to get shit right in there." He rubbed his shoulder as he talked then nodded his head at Ian. "Now your turn."

Ian raised a brow. "My turn for what?"

"I told you how I ended up here. Your turn to tell me why you did." Ian sat there quiet, his focus darting around the room, avoiding making eye contact because he had started to panic. "Hey, Ian, I'm sorry man. Didn't mean to push. If you don't wanna talk about what happened to you, I—"

Ian shook his head, halting Josh's words. "No, man, you're cool," he said. "It's just... You're the first person I've told, you know? Everybody here already knows. And my sister knew before I even did."

"You got a sister?" Josh asked, chugging some water. Ian nodded. "She hot?"

Ian couldn't help but laugh. Well, he just answered the *real* question Ian had been wanting to ask. "She's my sister, man," he said, still laughing. "You stay the hell away from her."

"Why?" Josh asked, pretending to be offended. "Because of my bum leg?" He even stuck his titanium addition out into the middle of the room and shouted, grabbing the attention of the few other people in therapy with them. Andrew smiled but went right back to what he had been doing.

"You're such a dork, dude," Ian said, shaking his head and smiling. "And no, because you're a big-ass player, I can already tell." Josh pretended to think about Ian's words for a second before nodding in agreement and laughing along with Ian. He drank more water and grew serious, his smiled fading.

"Seriously, though, Ian, if you don't wanna tell me, you don't have to."

Ian shifted on the bench. "I know, man, and I appreciate that. But... I gotta be able to tell people when they ask. And if I can't tell a complete stranger, then I got some issues." Josh cocked his head and stared at Ian as he dug deep to find the courage to say words he never thought he'd be fucking saying—not about himself.

"I, uh... I was jumped for being gay."

Josh's eyes grew wide. "Oh. Wow. I didn't know. Sorry, man. That...really sucks."

Ian laughed to ward off the uncomfortable fog suddenly hanging in the air between them. "Yeah, I guess. I mean, compared to going to fucking war, though? A gay bashing is no big deal."

"No way," Josh said with a shake of the head. "They don't even compare. What happened to me was because of something we were doing. Something *I* was doing. But what you went through, man?" He stopped, stared at Ian. "It's not right."

Ian smiled, though on the inside he had broken in half. Part of him wanted to get up and leave, never see Josh again because he felt so fucking embarrassed. But the other half, the stronger half, felt so touched by this stranger who showed him genuine concern.

"Thanks man," he said. "That means a lot."

"I don't pity you or anything," Josh said. "I mean every word. I hate people can't be who they are, you know? I mean, I've known you a few days now. And there are *so* many other reasons I'd wanna beat you up." He cut his eyes at Ian and busted out laughing. A roaring laughter so loud and happy and fucking carefree, Ian couldn't help but laugh too. "I'm just messing with ya, dude. You're pretty cool."

Ian tried to reign in his laughing fit. "Gee, Josh, thanks a lot," he said. "You're too damn kind." They kept laughing until the sound faded and Ian stood. He walked over and stuck out his hand. "Seriously though. Thanks man, means a lot to me."

Josh gave a nod and shook his hand. "Don't mention it, buddy."

Ian went back to his leg presses, feeling better about himself than he had in a long time.

Chapter Twenty-Six

Ian excelled at his physical therapy. By the end of the week he had doubled his total weight on the leg press and could walk up and down the halls on his floor like a champ. His spirits were up, he felt good about how far he had come, how far he could go, and he knew he'd be out of there in no time.

If he'd had a fucking clue, he would've seen the upset coming.

He had sweet-talked Elaine into taking him outside a couple of days ago by promising he'd let her teach him how to play something called Bridge, and now outside excursions had become part of their regular routine. On the days she worked, she would show up a half hour before his therapy appointment and wheel him to the small garden and courtyard area at the back of the hospital. On her days off, he got screwed. He had begged her to lose the chair and let him walk but she had flat out said no. He could tell pushing her wouldn't have worked so he bowed out and let her have her victory; he knew how to choose his battles to win a war.

Once outside, Ian got out of the chair and stood up and walked around a bit, soaking up the sun and the clean, refreshing air only a Chicago winter could bring. While others, Elaine included, were bundled up like they were in fucking Antarctica, Ian embraced the freezing winds and light snowfall. He could have stayed out there forever.

Until he saw Sam rounding the corner.

If he'd had the wheelchair next to him, he would've fallen into it. All the air left his lungs. His legs started to buckle. He felt dizzy. Wanted to pass the hell out. He somehow found the strength to stay standing as Sam walked up to him.

Sam seemed very timid, keeping a safe distance between them. He was clearly nervous and Ian didn't understand why. Ian himself had more than enough reasons to be nervous. He was the one standing in front of the one person he thought had abandoned him, turned away from him when he needed him the most.

"Hey, Ian," Sam said. Damn, he was so fucking hot Ian could feel his heart skip a beat. Sam wore a form-fitting black T-shirt and jeans, a black jacket, and a scarf around his neck. Sexy as hell and a good distraction for Ian from his own unsettling nerves.

"Uh... Hey." He had no clue what to say. Sam stood right there in front of him. In the flesh. Every fucking delicious inch of flesh. Two weeks ago, when he got Sam's Dear John letter, Ian thought he had just gotten Sam's official good-bye, the last time he would hear from him. At least until he got out of the hospital and could make the first move to get him back. But Sam had done a one-eighty, making the first move. Sam made the leap forward and now Ian could only try to figure out what the hell this all meant. "What are you doing here?"

"I... I just wanted to see you," Sam said. "You look good. Really good." His eyes wandered up and down Ian's body and for the first time Sam made Ian feel...off. Not bad, not good, just off.

A fucking tidal wave of shit ran through his head, crashing into the walls he had built around the memories of Sam to keep him at bay until Ian could get out and go see him. Sam here now, standing in front of him, overwhelmed him. Everything he felt right then, a world full of joy and pain and sadness and love, devoured him, leaving him empty and broken.

"Sam," he said, "I don't—what does this mean? You being here... Tell me what this means." Each word struggled to get out, ripping and tearing him apart. He had never been so scared to hear Sam's answer, no matter what said answer might be. Ian knew either way, his life would be different.

Sam kept his eyes locked on Ian. He didn't say anything at first, just stood there staring. The sun lit his blue eyes like stars, drawing Ian in like they had always done. Ian wanted to steer clear, hold back as long as he could to keep himself safe, but he'd never been able to resist the pull Sam's eyes had on him. They were the sun, Ian the planets, and he would be forever trapped in their orbit.

"I just wanted to make sure you were okay," Sam said. "I needed to know you were okay."

The air that had left his lungs when Sam first walked up came rushing back all at once. The force slammed into Ian's chest and rushed through his brain like a tornado, making his head spin. He opened his stance to keep from toppling over.

"You need to leave." Ian's words surprised them both. He never thought he would be saying something so crazy to Sam, no matter what they had or hadn't faced. Sam had always been his other half, the reason he kept going. To turn him away, he had to be fucking insane.

"Ian—" Sam stopped talking when Ian shook his head.

He couldn't open his eyes. Couldn't look Sam in the face. Couldn't see the pain there, the hurt. Seeing Sam hurt would be too much and he would give in. And he wasn't ready to give in just yet.

"I can't do this right now, Sam," he said. He took a deep breath and closed his eyes. Calmed himself down. Took a second before opening his eyes again. Sam's face held strong, but Ian knew him well enough to know he had to be feeling like shit inside. Ian knew the feeling, all too well. "I have to put myself first right now. I can't spare any part of me. I have to get better so I can get out of here. So, I can..." He couldn't bring himself to say the words out loud. To Sam. If he told Sam he planned on fighting to win him back, and Sam told him not to bother, he would be destroyed. He wasn't ready to face defeat yet. He had to get stronger, get out of the hospital. He needed to prepare for whatever might happen when he confronted Sam again.

When Sam turned away, Ian watched the muscles along his jaw roll beneath his skin, and knew he had to be gritting his teeth. Knowing he had hurt Sam obliterated his heart. Shattered the damn thing into a billion pieces. He never wanted to hurt Sam. Ever. Seeing him, though, after he said he wouldn't be back. Something inside Ian took over, forced him to push Sam away to save himself first.

"Good for you," Sam said, turning to face Ian again, his voice low and sad. So fucking sad. Ian's heart slammed against his chest. "I... I hope you get out of here soon."

Ian focused on Elaine, rocking back and forth on a tiny bench beneath a large, barren Dogwood tree. She caught him staring and pulled the headphones from her ears and stood up. He turned back to Sam.

"I have to go," he said. Elaine stood behind him with the wheelchair. He slid into the seat, trying not to wince as pain radiated across his body. He didn't want Sam to see him as weak. Elaine moved to take him back inside, but he stopped her. He and Sam locked eyes. "I'm sorry," he said, and Elaine wheeled him away.

Chapter Twenty-Seven

Ian started crying the second he turned around. As Elaine pushed him through the double doors at the back of the hospital and past the administration offices, janitorial department, and storage rooms, Ian rested his head in his hand and let the tears fall. His heart shattered over and over again, reliving the pain of pushing Sam away. For months Ian had been doing everything he could to get Sam, ignoring Sam's constant pleas for him to stop. But Ian hadn't stopped. Because he knew they were meant to be together, and he wouldn't stop for anything until Sam knew too. And now, after Sam had all but said he was done in his fucking letter, he showed up because he cared, and Ian shot him down.

What the hell was wrong with him?

The elevator dinged and the doors opened, and Ian snapped back to the present. Elaine pushed him toward the Therapy Center, the last fucking place he wanted to be. He conjured the nerve to tell her he planned on skipping therapy today and to just take him back to his room when Josh came out of the stairwell. Of course, Captain America would take the stairs, the showoff. He saw them before Ian had the chance to get out of there and headed their way, his bionic leg sticking out of his cargo shorts with well-deserved pride.

"Hey guys," he said, smiling. "How you doing today?"

Ian put on his best happy face. "Same old, same old," he answered, trying to match Josh's way-too-cheerful mood.

"We are wonderful, aren't we, sweetie?" Elaine piped up and patted Ian on the shoulder. "How are you not freezing, young man?" she said to Josh. "It's the apocalypse out there!"

"The colder the better," Josh said. "Cold air is good for ya." He held the door to the therapy room open for them and Elaine pushed Ian's wheelchair through.

"Oh, no," she said, locking Ian's wheels in place. "Give me a tropical island any day." She and Josh laughed, and Ian couldn't get away from them fast enough. He headed straight for the leg press and climbed aboard. He tuned out everything around him. Elaine and Josh's small talk, Andrew and the girl he busily taught how to pick things up again, the "positive" techno-style music. He tried to focus on his workout. He pushed the weights, now up to two hundred pounds, up and down, over and over, working up a sweat. His brain fought against him the entire time, bringing up thoughts and images of Sam and the letter and all the shit Ian had done to him. The more he saw, the harder he pushed.

"Take it easy there, bud. You're gonna hurt yourself."

Ian hadn't even noticed Josh jump on the weight bench next to him. He stopped mid-press, said," don't care," and finished out his set of twenty.

"All right, man, spill." Josh sat up on the bench and stared at Ian.

"Spill what?"

"I could tell something was up the second I saw you. I mean, you're never really in a good mood, but today you seem more upset than normal." Josh smiled, and even though his mood couldn't have been more opposite Ian smiled too. He swung his legs off the bench, ignoring the twinge of sharp pain running down each one.

"Sorry, man," he said, snagging a hand towel from the stack next to the machines and wiping sweat from his face. "I just... I've kind of had a tough morning."

"Need to talk?"

Did he? Ian hadn't wanted to even fucking *think* about Sam showing up or the fact he walked away from him for the second time.

"If not, no problem," Josh said, putting his hands up. "Just thought getting things off your chest might help."

"You sure I won't make you uncomfortable?"

Josh squinted. "How would you?"

"You know," Ian said. "You, me, talking about relationships..." Josh didn't seem to be catching on so Ian added, "And I'm gay?"

Josh smiled. "Dude, a relationship is a relationship. Gay, straight, somewhere in the middle, when they suck, they suck. We all run into problems, we all find ways to fix them. Who's standing there beside you doesn't matter."

Ian took in Josh's words. The guy oozed coolness, and seemed smarter and more in-tune than the average guy, but Ian hadn't expected him to be so open. His macho, military surface had been a front; he was a total teddy bear underneath.

Ian smiled. Nerves crawled up his back and he took a deep breath. He didn't want to open himself up to the pain he'd been fighting to move past since the day he got Sam's letter, but something uncontrollable grabbed hold of him and he poured his heart out before he could stop himself.

He told Josh everything. His parents dying. Skipping town in the middle of the night. The drugs and alcohol and all the stupid shit he'd done since coming back home. The more he said, the more he wanted to say. He couldn't have stopped the words even if he had wanted to. He felt so fucking good to be able to say how he felt about Sam after all this time to someone other than Rachel, who had been bound by blood to agree with whatever stupid decision he made. And Josh was right, he could listen with the best of them. He sat there and let Ian go through a gamut of emotions as he relived the past year or so, never growing tired or frustrated of hearing about somebody else's messed up life. When Ian finished, Josh leaned back on his hands.

"So this guy—Sam?—just showed up today out of the damn blue?" Ian nodded. "*After* he said he wasn't coming back?"

Ian nodded. "Right? That's why I acted so weird when I got here. Sorry if I was a dick."

Josh waved him off. "No more than usual," he said with a smile and Ian laughed.

"Gee, thanks." Josh shrugged and took a hit off his water bottle. "I know he said he just stopped by to see how I was doing," Ian continued, "but I don't know if I believe him."

"Oh, yeah, he's lying for sure," Josh said.

"You think so?"

"Guy tells you he's moved on, can't see you anymore, then later he shows up without telling you?" He stopped talking and Ian stared at him wide-eyed. "He missed you, man."

Ian ran his hands through his hair and huffed. "See why I'm so fucking frustrated?" he said. "All this time he's been pushing me away. I *finally* get to the point where I think, Okay, maybe I need to start listening to him. Leave him alone. Then this." He shook his head. "I just... I don't know what the hell to do."

"My advice? *Don't* start listening to him. If you want him back, you get him back."

Ian laughed. "Yeah, super simple."

"Tell me something," Josh said. "When you're around Sam, do you get a weird feeling in your gut? Like, you feel nervous and excited all at the same time?" Ian nodded. "I guarantee you Sam gets the exact same feeling around you."

Ian rolled his eyes. "Doubt it."

"When my girlfriend Stephanie and I broke up after almost two years, I got so messed up, man. Thought she was the one, you know? I became fucking *obsessed* with getting her back. I somehow got her to meet me one day, just to talk and see if we could fix our problems. And I couldn't wait, man. Like, this is my one shot. My one shot to get her back." He looked away for a second.

"Did you?" Ian asked.

"There's the thing," Josh said. "While we sat there talking, I realized I didn't want the same things anymore. I didn't want to get back together with her. I just didn't have those feelings anymore, you know?" He pressed a hand against his stomach. "The butterflies were gone. I spent so much time missing the relationship, missed the thought of *having* a relationship, I didn't even notice." He grabbed his water and stood up and walked over to Ian. "If you still feel all twisted up inside when you see Sam, believe me, he feels the same way. Otherwise he wouldn't have come back. He'd be gone already." He put his hand on Ian's shoulder and gave him a firm squeeze. "Don't give up, man. Trust me on this one. Don't give up." He turned and walked away, throwing a "see ya tomorrow" over his shoulder.

Since he had gotten Sam's letter, Ian had been trying to ignore the feeling in his gut, the one Josh had talked about. He wanted to be able to give Sam the respect he had been begging for and let him live his life. Now... So many things were running through his head. Should he leave Sam alone? Should he fight for him? Would Sam ever admit what he felt, if he felt anything at all? The endless questions were frustrating as hell, driving him insane. He wanted to believe what Josh said—shit, winning Sam back had been all he wanted since day one—but a part of him felt too scared to go down the same road again, to get rejected again if Sam pushed him away. The weight of doubt started pressing down on him like a million tons of bricks.

He shoved the endless what-ifs from his head and went back to pushing weights.

The one thing he could do without thinking.

Chapter Twenty-Eight

His day of freedom came faster than Ian had expected. His doctors all said he had begun healing better than they had hoped, and Andrew had been very impressed with how far he'd come on his therapy. He walked around the halls of the hospital every free second he had, broke two-twenty-five on the leg press, and even managed to add some definition to his arms after winning the fight and convincing Andrew he would look like a fucking chicken if he didn't.

All the work had been easy after Sam messed with his head by showing up unannounced. He didn't want to think about Sam or what his surprise drop-in meant or didn't mean, so he poured all his energy and focus into busting out of the prison disguised as a hospital. His efforts had paid off and he bounced on the edge of his bed like a sugar-loaded kid on Halloween while he waited for his ride to freedom. He had already said his good-byes to the nurses and doctors and therapists—Andrew even gave him a warm hug and said Ian had been the best patient he'd ever had, though Ian figured he said the same thing to everybody—and swapped contact info with Josh, both of them promising to keep in touch.

He also took Josh's advice, which is the main reason he wanted to get out of there. He needed to get to Sam, tell him just how he felt, what he wanted. The thought of taking such a big leap and putting himself out there again scared him shitless, but he couldn't give up. Because he knew Sam wanted the same thing. Even if doing so scared Sam to death too.

Elaine brought the wheelchair. Turned out the hospital had a stupid ass policy to roll patients through the entire place so everybody could get one last ogle in. Rachel carried his suitcase as they made their way outside. The Chicago winter had its game face on, snow falling thick and heavy with a strong, frigid wind blowing through. Elaine wrapped her arms around herself right after she set the brakes on the chair and complained about the cold; Ian reveled in the falling temperatures.

"I think I might miss you most, Elaine," Ian said after Rachel walked off to get the car. He had never been the touchy-feely, share all your emotions all the damn time type of guy, but somehow he had changed since waking up after almost dying. Now, he wasn't so tightlipped at the thought of telling people how he felt. He didn't plan on shouting I love you to every damn person he met, but he could at least tell Elaine what he thought of her. "You're pretty cool."

"Oh, I know I'll miss you, sweetie," Elaine said. She patted him on the arm, no doubt her favorite gesture of endearment since she did the same thing to everybody. "And if you don't mind a little advice from an old lady?" Ian gave her a smile and nodded.

"Hit me."

"Don't you let that boy get away." Her words caught him off guard. All this time, he thought she hadn't been listening, too busy rocking away to Bon Jovi or Aerosmith on her iPhone.

"How did you—you weren't even listening."

Elaine smiled and stared out over the parking lot. "I learned a long time ago how to not be seen or heard when I didn't need to be," she said. "I learned how to pretend to listen to music so people could have some privacy too." Her face was soft and sincere when she spoke. "Don't you waste any more time wondering if you should take a chance, son. If you get the opportunity to tell somebody you love just how *much* you love them, you take it. Don't you dare let the moment pass you by. Trust me, you don't want to live the rest of your life regretting *not* telling them."

Ian wondered what regrets she had but kept the thought to himself. He still couldn't believe she hadn't said something to him before, hadn't told him she overheard him begging Sam to leave. His heart opened up again, raw and throbbing. Elaine had been the second person in a week to tell him to not give up on trying to get Sam back; he figured maybe now he should listen. He already wanted to anyway, in his heart. He just had to convince his head to catch up.

Without overthinking things, without telling himself he had gone too far outside of his comfort zone and he needed to dial back a notch, Ian stood up out of his wheelchair and wrapped his arms around Elaine. Then he closed his eyes and just let her hug him back. He hadn't been hugged so honestly in so long. He took his time and enjoyed the warmth. The love. The feeling of *being* loved. He realized then just how much he had missed a human connection.

"Oh, sweetie," Elaine said, putting her hand against the side of his face. "You take good care of yourself, you hear me?" Ian nodded as tears streaked his face. "And you come back to see us whenever you want. But only as a visitor, now. You better not show up here as a patient again." They both laughed and Ian held on longer than necessary before he broke their hug. Elaine brought both hands up this time and held tight to his face. Ian closed his eyes for a second to take in the warmth of them.

"And you remember what I said," she told him. "Don't let a chance pass you by. I don't want you regretting anything in forty years, crying about your shoulda, woulda, couldas. You just have to"—she took her hands from his face and curled them into fists—"grab your opportunities by the balls whenever you can and hold on tight."

Ian laughed through his tears and gave her another quick hug as Rachel pulled up next to them. She came around to the passenger side of the car and opened his door, standing by while he stayed in Elaine's arms.

"I lied," he said, staring into Elaine's teary eyes and smiling. "I *know* I'm gonna miss you most."

*

Ian and Rachel were quiet as they headed home. Rachel stayed focused on keeping the car on the snowy road while Ian stared out the window, going over and over what both Josh and Elaine had said. They made things sound so fucking simple, as if taking a chance and going after what you want is as common as breathing. But he knew the truth would be so much harder, so much more complex. He was living proof how being stubborn and determined didn't always win. Hell, he had been trying to get Sam to wake up and see he still loved Ian since the moment Ian had gotten back into town and nothing had happened. He didn't know if he had the strength to go through the struggle and pain again.

One thing he did know, though? He wasn't anywhere near ready to say good-bye to Sam. Sam had his heart, all the fractured, mangled pieces, and Ian couldn't imagine life without him. Which made this so damned hard. And scared the shit out of him. If he kept pushing, Sam would cut him out of his life for good. And never seeing Sam again would destroy him.

He tried to push the thoughts to the back of his mind, their relentless badgering giving him one killer of a headache. He smiled at Rachel and felt the part of his heart she held, the only part not broken, swell. His sister was the fucking best. Through all the shit, and there had been *a lot*, she had been there for him when no one else had. Stood by him when others bailed. All his life, Ian knew he could count on her, knew she would always be there to pick him up when he fell. And he had fallen a lot. A thousand more times than most people. But every single time Rachel had been there, helping him off the floor and back to his feet. She meant more than the world to him.

"What?" Rachel said when she caught him staring. "Do I have something on my face?" She kept her eyes on the road and a tight grip on the wheel as her sedan cut through the snow. The rate of snowfall had more than doubled since they'd left the hospital, and visibility neared nonexistent levels. Ian could feel the slide and pull of the car as the tires found their way through the muck.

"No, you dork," he said. "I just... I love you, Rach. I really wanted you to know."

She smiled and risked their safety to glance over at him. "I love you too, baby brother," she said with a big grin plastered on her face.

"Thank you," Ian said, his voice soft, tender. "For everything." The emotions he had been fighting off started bubbling up and he focused on the scenery out his window again so Rachel wouldn't see his eyes filling with tears. Damn, he had turned into a faucet he cried so fucking much. "I know I don't say thanks enough. Or not at all, probably." He kept blinking to make his tears go away. "I, uh, just wanted to make sure you knew how much I appreciate all you've done for me. *Do* for me." He turned when he heard her sniffle. "Crap, I'm sorry. I didn't mean to make you cry."

Rachel shook her head and took one hand off the wheel to wipe her face. "No, no, don't be," she said. "This is happy crying." She smiled at him. "I'm happy crying. I promise. And you know I love you more than anything, Ian. And I am so happy I've been able to be there when you've needed me." She smiled at him and added, "I'll never not be."

Ian took a deep breath and exhaled slowly, forcing his nerves out of his throat where they had been holding on for dear life. "Could I ask you for a favor?" he asked.

"Shoot."

"Instead of going straight home, I kinda hoped, maybe..."

Rachel glanced over when he stopped talking. "What?" she asked. "You wanna stop to eat or something, or..." She nodded and smiled when she got what he didn't say. "Ah. Of course," she said with a wry smile and a nod. "Sam."

Chapter Twenty-Nine

By the time Rachel pulled into the animal shelter where Sam worked, Ian's frantic nerves were wound up so tight he thought he would snap. He'd had no clue if Sam would be there or not when he had made the decision to grab life by the balls, as Elaine had suggested, and go see him right away, so he let out his pent up breath when he spotted Sam's car in the lot. He had made the decision to track Sam down on impulse, something he maybe should have thought about longer than the thirty seconds before he asked his sister to bring him there. But he hadn't, and now he sat outside Sam's work, trying to find the courage to get out and go inside. A few days ago he had all but told Sam to leave him alone. Now he planned to go in there and beg the man to take him back. He confused even himself.

"Are you sure you wanna do this, Ian?" Rachel asked. She still had her hands on the wheel even though they weren't moving, and Ian wondered if she felt nervous for him too. Hell, she should be; he felt like a fucking idiot right then. "We can turn around and go home if—"

"No," Ian interrupted, shaking his head. He grabbed the handle and opened the door, flooding the car with icy air. "I have to do this. Now." He got out of the car and slammed the door shut. His legs ached and his back screamed at him after sitting for so long, but he ignored the pain.

"I'll wait here," Rachel called out behind him. He turned and headed to her side of the car.

"Don't," he said. "Don't wait for me. I'll be fine."

"Ian, you can barely walk. You'll never make it all the way home by foot."

"Don't worry, I won't try to walk home. I'll call a cab. Or you can come pick me up later. I just...I need to talk to Sam, and I won't be able to, knowing you're sitting out here waiting for me."

"Are you sure?" she asked, and Ian nodded. "Okay, I'll leave. But promise me you'll call me if you need me to come back."

"I promise." Ian smiled and headed toward the shelter. He knew he wouldn't call Rachel to pick him up because she would have to trudge back out in the snow, and she fucking *hated* the cold and the snow and especially *driving* in snow. So he would find his own way home. He didn't have time to worry about getting how now, though, because he needed to focus on what he would say to Sam when he saw him.

He took his time crossing the gravel parking lot, the rocks rolling and shifting beneath his feet and the snow acting more like quicksand, threatening to bring him down like a towering pine tree with every step. His legs were stronger than they had been when he first started physical therapy, but they were nowhere near where he wanted them to be. The last thing he needed was to rebreak them for being a clumsy idiot. After what felt like an hour but in reality hadn't been more than two minutes, Ian stepped onto the porch of the shelter and out of the snow and stood there with his hand on the doorknob for forever before he got the nerve to go inside.

"Hi," the lady behind the desk said. She either didn't recognize him from last time or she pretended not to. "Interested in adoption today?"

"Uh, no," Ian said. "I'm…here to see Sam. Is he busy?" He had some serious déjà vu when her voice came over the loudspeaker calling Sam to the lobby and he walked over to the same corner he had sat in when he had been here before. He stood this time, next to the same dirty fake tree, since his legs were aching like a bitch and sitting only made them hurt worse. He didn't have to wait long though, because Sam came through the door a few seconds later and Ian's heart leapt into his fucking throat. Jesus, just the sight of Sam mixed him all up every single time he saw him, and this time felt no different. He became nervous and scared and excited when Sam gave him a small smile.

"Hey," Sam said as he shoved his hands into his back pockets. The move pulled his T-shirt tight against his chest and Ian could see the muscular pecs and abs under the lifted fabric. He forced himself to turn away. "You look great," Sam added. "Glad to see you out of the hospital."

"Thanks," Ian said. "Not a hundred percent yet but definitely getting there."

Sam smiled again. "You will." An awkward moment of silence tried to shove a wedge between them. but Sam spoke again and the wedge shattered into a million shards. "Any word on if the police found who jumped you?" he asked.

Ian shook his head. "No leads, apparently. They might never catch them."

Sam's smile faded. "They will, one day."

Ian gave a half-hearted smile back. "Hey, uh, could we maybe go somewhere and talk?" He stuck his own hands in his pockets to keep Sam from seeing them shake.

"Yeah, sure." Sam looked over his shoulder to the woman behind the desk. "Hey, Jess, I'll see ya later?" Jess nodded and smiled and went back to doing whatever she had been doing. "I know it's cold, but there's not really anywhere private in here, so…" Sam gestured to the front door.

"No problem," Ian said. He started for the door, but Sam stopped him.

"You sure?" he asked, stealing a quick glance at Ian's legs. "There's a lot of snow out there."

Ian eyed his legs too. "Oh. Yeah." He laughed a little. "I'm good." He didn't wait for Sam to pity him anymore and walked outside.

The air felt colder than it had a few minutes ago, like the temperature was on a steady decline. Any other time the cold wouldn't have bothered him, but he felt the chill in his bones now. Just one more thing forever altered since he'd been beaten damn near to death. He ignored the shivers racking his body, knowing his blood pressure would go up as soon as he started talking to Sam and he would be warm as fire.

"I think I have an extra coat in my car if you need one," Sam said, zipping up his own. Ian hadn't even seen him grab the thick jacket from the hook by the door on their way out.

"I'm fine," Ian lied. He wasn't fine. Very fucking far from fine. Scared to death he was about to mess things up for good described him better. He just knew he would screw up and push Sam so far away he would never get him back. "Sam, I—"

"Me first," Sam interrupted. He led them over to the end of the farm-style fence and leaned against the post. "I wanted to apologize for stopping by the hospital unannounced the other day. I shouldn't have just shown up without calling you first."

"Oh. Okay. Thanks." An apology had been the last thing Ian expected. He went there intending to do all the apologizing. Sam's atonement threw him off a bit. "But you don't need to apologize for anything, Sam. I—I'm the one who's sorry." Ian shifted his weight, trying to take a little pressure off his legs.

Sam cocked a brow. "For what?"

"I'm sorry for a lot of shit," Ian said. He gripped the railing next to him, squeezing the rough wood so hard his fingers hurt. He welcomed the quick, sharp pain because pain helped him ignore the fear trying to shut him up. "I'm sorry for pushing you away the other day. I was... I didn't want you to go. Not really. I just—I didn't know what to think because of your letter and—"

"God, Ian, I never meant to get you upset."

Ian held out a hand to stop him. "Wait. Please. Let me say this." He took a deep breath. Held the breath tight in his lungs until his chest burned and seized before exhaling. "I never should've left. Back then, I mean. I was fucking stupid." He turned and rested his arms on the top rung of the fence and stared out over the empty dog pens filling up with snow. "So fucking stupid."

Sam laughed. "Wow," he said. "Is that it?" His defensive tone caught Ian's attention and he turned to face him. "You walk out on me, disappear without an explanation for over a year, and all you can say is sorry, I'm just stupid?"

"No." Ian shook his head. "No, this is not how I wanted this to sound. I just—Shit, this ain't going how I planned." He let go of the fence and rubbed his face. He had fucked this up and he hadn't even been there ten minutes. A personal record.

"What *did* you plan, Ian? How did you think this would go? You would come here, talk sweet to me, tell me how sorry you are, and I would, what? Say okay, let's get back together?"

Ian shrugged. "I don't know," he said. "I didn't think things would go *exactly* how you said." He sure as hell had hoped Sam would forgive him and jump into his arms and they would live happily ever after, though he knew the odds were more than stacked against him. "I thought maybe, after all this time, after all the times I've apologized for being such an idiot, you would at least think about trying to find a way to maybe forgive me." He pulled his eyes away from Sam and stared at his feet. He dragged them back and forth through the snow, scared as hell what Sam would say.

"I forgave you a long time ago," Sam said. "But forgiveness doesn't mean I forgot what you did."

Ian hadn't realized he held his breath again until air flew out of his lungs in a mad rush, carrying some of his fear too. Sam forgave him. He couldn't believe Sam fucking forgave him. Finally, a step in the right direction. "Thank you," he said, nodding. "Thank you for forgiving me. And I understand why you can't forget what I did. I can't forget what I did either. I'll never fucking forget. But... The past doesn't change the fact I still love you, Sam. And I know you still love me."

Sam rolled his eyes. "Jesus, Ian, you have to stop doing this. We can't keep playing this game."

"I'm not giving up on us, Sam. I can't. I thought I should after I read your letter. Hell, I had just about talked myself into it. But then you showed up at the hospital and... Well, you changed everything."

"I told you already, I shouldn't have come. I made a mistake."

"No, you didn't," Ian said, shaking his head. He stepped closer to Sam and tried to hold his hand, but Sam pulled away. "You trying to deny what you really feel is the mistake," he went on. "You know you still love me. I wish you'd just admit that. Just *say* you do so we can move on. Please, Sam. Don't keep holding us back—"

"Jesus, okay!" Sam threw his arms in the air. Spun around. Ran his fingers through his curls, the snow captured there crashing to the white ground at his feet. He was fighting mad when he spoke again. "I still love you, Ian. Is that what you want to hear? Yes, I still love you."

Chapter Thirty

Hearing Sam bite the bullet and admit what Ian had known all along knocked the breath out of him. He fell back against the fence, the aged wood rocking beneath his weight. Months of denying the truth, denying his true feelings, and Sam finally said the words.

He still loved Ian.

Sam checked his watch. "Crap, I gotta get going," he said, stepping past Ian toward the parking lot in a rush.

Ian pulled himself away from the fence and stood upright. "*Now*?" he asked. "Now you're gonna leave? Why?"

Sam stopped and turned back to him. "I—I can't be here anymore. I have to get home. Noah's waiting."

Ian laughed. "Of course. Noah. Can't forget about Noah." Anger rose from deep inside him, raw and enraged and clawing to be let out and he gripped the fence again to try to stop the spinning.

Sam's shoulders dropped. "Don't, Ian," he said. "Don't be this way."

Ian glared at him. "What way?"

Sam took a second before making eye contact again. "Don't force me to say something I didn't want to say and then get mad when I want to leave."

Ian laughed. "Are you serious right now? I didn't force you to say anything. You said how you feel because you faced what you've known since I showed up at your house the night I came back to town. You still love me. *Me*, Sam. Not the asshole you're running home to."

Sam laughed this time. "Ah, there we go. You're jealous."

"I'm not jealous I'm pissed off," Ian said through gritted teeth. "There's a big fucking difference." The rage boiling inside him inched up to the surface and Ian was so scared he wouldn't be able to stop himself from unleashing.

"Is there?" Sam asked. "Jealousy and anger usually go hand in hand."

Ian smiled and shook his head. "Whatever, doesn't matter. You love me, and now you're scared as shit so you're running away."

Sam narrowed his eyes. "Well if anybody would know what running away looks like it would be you." His words were like a second slap to Ian's face. They stung and burned because they were true.

And Ian knew Sam had been dead-on and he fucking hated himself. He hated himself because he knew, deep down, he should have left things alone. He shouldn't have said anything. He should have kept his damn mouth shut when Sam said he still loved him. Sam's words were what he had been dying to hear all this time and he had gotten what he'd wanted. But he never knew when to quit. As far back as he could remember he always pushed and pushed until he got what he wanted when he wanted, the instant gratification all kids crave regardless of the long-term outcome. And even now as an adult he still couldn't let go of getting his way when he wanted and how he wanted. Only now, the risk was a hell of a lot higher than an extra piece of candy or an extra hour added to his curfew. He watched Sam cross the snow-covered lot heading toward his car and without even thinking he took off after him.

He couldn't run, not like he used to anyway, but he walked as fast as his still-healing legs would let him. He ignored the snow, the loose gravel, the lumps and divots in the dirt. He didn't give a shit if he fell and broke a leg, broke both of them. He only cared about stopping Sam.

"Sam! Wait!" he called out just as Sam opened the door of his car. The frigid wind pouring in off the great lake didn't make the situation any easier as he walked, his body shivering as the powerful gusts tried to toss him off his feet. He slid and pivoted on the snow-covered rocks littering the parking lot, but he kept focused, determined. The temperature kept dropping, getting lower and lower by the minute, but Ian's blood drag-raced through his veins so fast he ignored the cold. He finally reached Sam's car. He watched as the wind lifted the curls framing Sam's face and tossed them around like little rings of pure fucking heaven, driving Ian crazy.

"Ian," Sam started, but Ian didn't give him the chance to finish. He took Sam in his arms and kissed him hard, frozen breath circling them in cloudy tendrils as he huffed and moaned, the throes of Heaven and Hell as the pain he felt after trying to run collided with the bliss kissing Sam created. His hands circled Sam's back, pulling them closer until their bodies crashed into each other as Ian's tongue stole the warmth inside Sam's mouth. An explosion went off inside him, creating toxic levels of rabid heat desperate to be assuaged.

Sam's mouth tasted like sweet summer strawberries and mint and Ian couldn't get enough. He had missed the taste. The smell of Sam. The feeling of their bodies pressed so tight together you couldn't fit a sheet of paper between them if you tried as they made out in the falling snow. He didn't want the moment to end. Didn't want a life without Sam, without kissing him. Or having Sam kiss him back, which Sam did with wild abandon.

Sam's tongue wrestled with Ian's. Fought for control. Devoured every crevice of Ian's mouth. Tiny whimpers escaped him, sending Ian over the edge. He gave two fucks they were in the middle of a parking lot, right out for everybody to see. He wanted Sam. More than he ever had. He slid a hand around Sam's waist. Down his abs. Gripped his crotch. Felt the hardness there.

"Stop," Sam said through the kiss, though his lips had yet to get the message. "God, please stop." Ian didn't back down, kept sweeping inside Sam's mouth with his tongue until Sam broke their kiss and pulled his face away. His hands were on Ian's chest, first clawing like a wild animal, desperate to reach inside and caress Ian's heart, then pushing him away. Ian stared at the lips he had just been gorging himself on. They were wet. Plumped. Inviting. With everything inside him, he wanted to taste them again. He wanted to ignore Sam's hands pressing into his pecs in protest and just fucking go for gold. He restrained himself though and bit his own swollen bottom lip until he felt pain. His breath came in ragged spurts. Heaving. His hands were still on Sam's hips and he could feel the electricity pulsing through his entire body. Sam felt alive, like an exposed nerve of want and sexual energy, and his overbearing need drove Ian fucking crazy.

"Don't fight this," Ian whispered as he inched closer and closer. "Don't fight what you know you want. What you know is meant to be. You and me, Sam. It's always gonna be you and me."

"Stop, Ian. I can't. We can't do this. I'm—I'm with Noah."

Well, those words will kill a boner faster than shit. Ian pulled his fingers from inside the waistband of Sam's jeans and dropped his arms. The rage came back, shattering the euphoria he and Sam had worked up like glass.

"Fuck!" he yelled, spinning around and dragging his hands through his hair. Sam jumped, his own chest heaving from their impromptu make-out session. Ian became a melting pot of emotions. Lust, want, anger, desire; they were all there, coiling in on each other, becoming a giant ball of energy threatening to consume him.

Fucking Noah. The half-naked asshole who had taken Sam from him. *He* was the reason Sam couldn't see how much he still loved Ian. How much he still wanted him. Sam *knew* he still loved Ian, he didn't doubt that anymore; he just wouldn't let himself *feel* the love he had for Ian. All because of his loyalty or kindness or some other fucked up, stupid reason. Ian never wanted to rip somebody's head off their shoulders more.

"Fuck him," he said, turning back to Sam. "Fuck Noah. He doesn't mean shit, Sam. You and me. Nothing else matters." His arms were like tendrils, desperate to touch the man he loved. They slid back around Sam's waist, pulling him close again. "Drop him," he said, leaning in to kiss Sam again.

"No," Sam said, gripping Ian's arms and forcing him back. "Don't."

Ian stepped back. "Why not? You don't love him, Sam, can't you at least admit the truth? I can see you don't love him. Not like you love me. Why can't you see what I see? I mean, he's a hot fuck, I'm sure. But a fuck is all he is." His former asshole self came roaring back with a vengeance and Ian didn't even try to pretend otherwise. Desire had taken over, and he fucking loved the feeling. He had become the Ian he used to be. Before the beating which almost killed him. For the first time since waking up in the hospital he felt alive.

Sam's hand flew across his face before Ian knew what had even happened. The sting from the slap shot through his already wired body like a surge of electricity. A small laugh escaped Ian's throat as he rubbed his cheek.

"Oh, I can totally do rough," he said, his eyes wild with need.

"Fuck you, Ian," Sam spat back. "Five minutes ago things were good between us. Right where they needed to be after everything. All you've done to screw us up. Now you come over here and screw everything up a*gain*."

Ian's breath caught in his throat and his stomach rolled. The one thing he had hoped like hell he wouldn't do, fuck things up again, happened, and he didn't know how to stop himself.

"I knew," Sam said, shaking his head. "The night you showed up at my house, I knew I should have just walked away. I never should have let you back into my life." He made eye contact with Ian. "This is all my fault. Everything since the other night is my fault." He had been holding onto the open car door but let his hand fall away as he stepped closer to Ian. "I'm so sorry, Ian, if me showing up at the hospital the other day confused you. Or what I just said did. Or kissing you. God, I never meant to make you think this is what I wanted. Because...I don't. I meant what I said in my letter. I've moved on." Ian had trouble making out the words Sam spewed because all he could hear were his hopes shattering.

But he wouldn't give up. Not yet.

"Don't say such bullshit," he said, reaching out to touch Sam but stopping short. He brought his hand back to his side. "You love me, Sam. You just said the words, but... Can you *feel* them? Can you feel the hunger, deep down inside you?" He brought his hand up to Sam's chest. Let his fingers rest there, relishing the heat. He couldn't resist. He had to feel Sam's heart pounding as much as he needed air to breathe, signaling the truth Sam so desperately tried to deny. Sam didn't move, didn't pull away from Ian's touch. "Your heart is beating a mile a minute right now," Ian said. "The crazy, haywire feeling in your chest? It's because of me, Sam. Seeing me. Touching me. *Kissing me.* You can say no all day long, but you want this. Just as much as I do."

Sam stood silent forever before he slid his hand over Ian's. Ian smiled—until Sam pushed his hand away. "I *did* want this," Sam whispered; tears coated his words. "I wanted you back. I did. I wanted to be enough for you. I wanted you to love me like you promised you would."

"You *are* enough," Ian said, pleading in his voice. "And I *do* fucking love you. I can't even put into words how much I love you."

Sam shook his head. "I don't think you even know what love means anymore, Ian. What loving somebody means. You're... just too broken to know." Sam stared at him, deep into his eyes, and Ian couldn't mistake the pain and despair swimming in those gorgeous blue pools. Sam's sadness burned like acid on his heart.

"Maybe you're right," Ian said. "Maybe I don't know what loving someone really means. But it doesn't fucking matter. Because I know what I *want*. And I want *you*, Sam. I want to be with you. I want to be *us*. Forever."

Sam threw his arms in the air. "Forever?" he asked. "Or until something bad happens again and you disappear and I have to start all over? Like last time?"

"I told you how sorry I was about leaving," Ian snapped. "My parents had just fucking *died*, Sam. I...I couldn't deal." Ian's heart ripped in half at the thought of his parents, every tear pooling in his eyes like knives in his chest. His gut. His throat.

"I know," Sam said with a whisper. "And I'm so, so sorry. But...bad things happen, Ian. I mean, that's what life is. A bunch of bad things separated by a few good. You don't get to run away and hide every time you're hurt or scared or sad. Not when you have somebody beside you, going through the bad with you.

My heart *broke* when your parents died. Because their deaths killed *you*. But I stayed, right there, waiting for you to come through your pain, waiting to *help* you through your pain. But you... You left. You chose to *leave*. Leave *me*." Sam stopped talking. He tried to hide as he wiped tears from his face and Ian's shredded heart wanted to jump out of his fucking chest. "I don't know if I can ever forgive you for leaving," Sam added, refusing to make eye contact. "I know I said I had, but..."

"Sam—"

Sam shook his head and eyes were filled with tears. "Don't," he said. "Please. Don't." Sam stood quiet. Stared at Ian. Almost reached out to touch him before drawing his hand back to his side. "I—I have to go." He stepped away from Ian and Ian felt like the world had finally slipped away from him. He couldn't move, couldn't breathe. He could only stand there helpless, silent, paralyzed as Sam gripped the door to his car. "I'm sorry, Ian," Sam went on. "I truly am. I'm sorry you're in so much pain. I'm sorry I can't love you the way you want me to. I'm sorry I can't be the man you want me to be. Or need me to be." He stayed silent again, the tears in his eyes giving up the losing battle and falling down his cheeks. He opened his mouth to speak. Choked back his words. Ian's eyes were glued to Sam. He blinked away tears so he could focus, so he wouldn't dare miss a second of Sam's perfect, beautiful face. He watched Sam struggle to speak. Watched him shake his head, lower his eyes and white-knuckle the car door before taking one last look at Ian again.

"I'm sorry you left," Sam said through his tears. Then he climbed into his car and drove away.

Chapter Thirty-One

Ian had no idea how long he had been standing in the parking lot of the animal shelter after Sam had driven away. Snow piled an inch high on his shoulders and the top of his head, so he must have been idle a while. He didn't care though. The snow could have buried him. Devoured him. He was destroyed. Completely, fully destroyed. Sam had told him he loved him. Had kissed him with so much passion the force left Ian breathless. Then he left. Sam still left knowing he didn't want to. Out of fear or some obligation to Noah, Ian didn't know. The reason didn't matter, only the fact Ian had lost him all over again.

Still in a daze, he started walking. He didn't notice the pain in his legs. Not at first. He made his way to the end of the street before the throbbing and aching running up his back brought him out of the mind-numbing fog Sam had left him in. He knew he would never reach home, not with the snow falling heavier now, but to be honest he didn't really give a shit. He didn't care about going home. He just wanted to sit on the side of the road and let the cold take him until he didn't feel the pain in his legs or back or heart anymore. He just wanted to make everything go away.

He settled on the next best way to feel numb.

He had made it to just over a mile away from Final Draft, but the walk took Ian almost twenty minutes. The thick layer of snow coating the sidewalks didn't help at all, his pace slow and awkward since his legs felt like they weren't attached to his body anymore. The feeling of being legless made him think of Josh and how much Ian wished he lived closer so they could talk. Maybe meet up. He thought about texting his new friend because he needed someone to unload on other than Rachel because he'd unloaded way more than enough on her, but left his phone in his pocket because no fucking way did he want to have one more person in this world feeling sorry for him.

Even though he knew deep down in his heart Sam didn't mean to, Ian could almost *see* the pity dripping from his words earlier. As if the pain of having Sam turn him down yet again wasn't enough, he had to face him knowing Sam pitied him too? Felt fucking sorry for him? The realization pissed him off.

Ian's anger morphed into hysterical laughter because his emotions were a fucking tangled mess as he rounded the corner and saw the sign for Final Draft swinging from a black wrought iron frame in the bitter Chicago wind. He suddenly got very excited to fucking plant his ass on a barstool and drink himself to death just so he wouldn't have to *feel* any fucking more. If someone had asked him a few months ago to sit around and share his feelings, he would've punched said someone in the fucking face. Now, after being jumped by some gay-hating pieces of shit, he wished for the chance. Jesus, he was a fucking mess.

He stepped inside Final Draft and smiled. And not a fake, half-assed, aww-I'm-so-sorry-to-hear-your-bad-news smile but a real, genuine smile because he felt a tiny sliver of happiness. Go fucking figure how happiness could even be possible since he felt like shit. The warmth smacked him in the face right along with all the smells the run-down place carried, and Ian had never felt more at home. His legs were ready to buckle beneath him from the abuse he had put them through all day, so he grabbed the first open barstool he came to and plopped down. The bar didn't seem too busy, a few regulars mixed with some faces Ian didn't recognize, and he thought of how perfect the place felt. When life had beaten you down so fucking low you didn't care if you lived or died, you needed to be around others who shared in your suffering. And there were none sadder and more depressing than the stragglers who hung around a bar until closing time.

"Oh my God." Ian heard Stacey's voice from the other end the bar. She lifted the hinged opening and made a beeline for Ian, reaching up and throwing her arms around his neck. "Are you okay?" she asked when she stepped back a few seconds later. "I heard about what happened. I can't even believe it. I swear to God, if I find out who the hell hurt you—"

Ian interrupted her ranting with a shallow laugh. "Thanks, Stacey," he said. "But don't get in trouble over me."

"Oh, I wouldn't. They'd never know I did a thing." She gave him a wink and went back behind the bar. He watched her stop by the draft station and fill a mug of the cheapest thing on tap. His mouth watered when she slid the frothy concoction in front of him.

"On the house," she said with a smile.

"All night?" He winked back.

"Don't push your luck, Mister." Stacey's words almost made Ian laugh. Luck? Shit, if he had made a list of things in his life Ian had none of, luck would at the top. Stacey went back to busying herself with wiping down the bar top and Ian wrapped his hand around the glass. Just the simple touch, his fingers caressing the frosted sides of the mug, calmed him. Soothed him. Eased the tiniest fraction of his pain. The condensation already built up soaked into his skin, the cold from the icy brew inside the glass making his fingers tingle. He hadn't had a drink since the night he got beaten up, so he wanted to savor every fucking second.

As soon as the froth touched his lips, he lapped up the sweet nectar like a starved dog put in front of a bowl of food. He inhaled half the glass before coming up for air, feeling the liquid gold flow all the way down his throat. He closed his eyes and wallowed in the euphoria. By the time he reached the bottom of the glass the fringes of a good buzz had started tickling his mind. Stacey had a second pint at the ready, and she kept them coming one after the other. Within minutes, all the shit Ian had been through in the past year had been drowned out and he felt nothing.

*

He managed to make his way back to Rachel's in one piece, puke- and piss-free. Considering how drunk he had gotten, he impressed himself. And he was almost wasted enough to forget about Sam and all the mess happening between them. Of course, forgetting could never *really* happen—not enough alcohol in the state to erase *that* memory—but he would settle for even five fucking minutes of peace. Five minutes without crying. Or missing Sam. Or wishing he had been in the backseat the night some asshole got the bright idea to drive a fucking car while wasted and killed his parents. Ian almost laughed at the irony. His parents' deaths had destroyed him, broken him into a million irreparable pieces, yet he had become the very thing that took them from him. If he wasn't so done-in over Sam, he might have appreciated the irony. He wouldn't have fucking cared one way or the other, but he would have appreciated it. He liked to drink. Liked ignoring his problems. Liked not feeling anything past numb. He had missed being numb.

The snow had let up a bit, but the already cold night had plummeted into danger-level temperatures. Even with the amount of liquor running through his veins, Ian felt cold as shit. He didn't feel any pain in his legs, though, which helped him navigate his way home faster than he would've thought. He didn't *want* to go home—he wanted to spend the rest of his life sitting at the bar—but fatigue had moved in to stay. A day of trying to drown his feelings had wiped him out and he just wanted to crash. He took his time climbing the icy porch steps and opened the door. Rachel sat in the living room just to the right of the entryway, staring Ian down when he came in.

"What?" he asked, rubbing his arms to try to warm up. "Jesus, it's fucking cold out there."

"Stacey called," she said. "We need to talk." She didn't get up. Didn't smile or roll her eyes or make some smartassed comment about his coming home drunk for the hundredth time. Her lack of emotion freaked him the fuck out.

"God, what now, Rach? You're fucking relentless, you know it?" He complained but still made his way over to the couch and plopped down. His head spun like a top, so he sunk into the back of the sofa and closed his eyes.

"What are you *doing*, Ian?" Rachel asked. She sat quiet for so long he had almost dozed off.

"What're you talking about? I'm not doing anything. Just having a good time."

"Oh, is *this* what a good time is? The same day out of the hospital and you're out getting drunk all day and night so you don't have to deal?"

Ian threw his arms up in frustration. "Deal with what? There's nothing to fucking deal with. I'm...all good." He just wanted to pass out, not have to listen to his sister's shit in the middle of the night.

"Okay, here's the thing, Ian. You're *not* good. You're a mess. I don't know why you can't see that." Ian didn't bother lifting his head or even opening his eyes, just flipped her off. "I looked everywhere for you," she said, ignoring him. "I went back to the shelter, but they said you must've left when Sam did. I drove up and down every street within five miles thinking you were in a ditch somewhere. Or worse. God only knows why I didn't think you would be at the goddamn bar." She stopped talking for a second and Ian thought the lecture portion of his night had ended until she started in again.

"Okay, I know you don't want to hear any of this," she went on, "I understand. But you have *got* to move on. You're a young, single, good-looking guy. You should be out enjoying your life."

"God. *Finally*. Thank you for finally fucking getting me. Now chill the hell out already."

"Ian, look at me." Jesus, she would. Not. Quit. Ian figured he might as well just give in because he knew she sure as hell wouldn't. He huffed but sat up on the couch and gave his full attention. "You are not having fun," she said. "This is not what fun is."

He laughed. "What're you talking about? I'm having a fucking blast."

"No, you're hiding."

"Hiding? From who? Sam?" More laughter. "I am not hiding from Sam, trust me. I'm not fucking scared of him."

"Hiding from everything," Rachel said. "Sam. What happened to you? Your addiction."

"I am *not* a fucking addict." Rachel pissed him off, ruining his trip back down.

"You need to process their deaths, Ian." Those words snapped him back. Ian's entire body tensed up, tightened, like a vise crushing him.

"Mom and Dad?" he asked, his brain trying to process what the hell she might be up to. "Are you fucking serious right now, Rachel? They died over a fucking year ago, and you wanna talk about them *now*?"

"They died over a year ago and you ran away. Disappeared. Doing God knows what. Then you show back up and you're..." Rachel's voice trailed off and her face tightened. Her eyes welled up. Tears fell from them, seared her cheeks. "You're broken, Ian. You're just...broken. Which scares the hell out of me more than anything."

"My God, I am *fine*. Seriously. Stop crying."

"No, you're not! You're not okay. Jesus, will you just stop trying to bullshit me and listen? You are killing yourself because you're too damned scared to face the fact they're gone."

Ian shot off the couch, rage consuming him. He clenched and unclenched his fists over and over to the point his fingers ached, and the skin of his palms felt raw. He stood only inches from his sister, fighting like hell against the unyielding rage inside him.

"You don't think I fucking know they're gone?!" he screamed, staring into her teary eyes. "I know they're dead, Rachel. I know *every. Fucking. Day*. Goddammit!" He cried now too. Which pissed him off even more because the whole point of what he had been doing with his life the past year, the drinking himself stupid and the drug use and sleeping with anyone who would have him, was so he wouldn't have to face shit anymore. Wouldn't have to cry anymore. Wouldn't have to *feel* anymore. "Fuck. I swear, I don't know what the hell you want from me." Rachel reached out to him, but Ian held out his arms to keep her away.

"Don't fucking touch me, Rachel. *Don't*." He fucking hated himself, crying like some weak loser. His parents were dead. And they had been. For a long time. So, crying over them now felt stupid and pointless.

Rachel ignored him, his defensiveness, inching closer and closer to him. "You know they're gone," she said, emotions squeezing her words like Death's grip, "but you haven't *dealt* with their deaths yet. You haven't *accepted* they're gone."

Ian wiped tears from his face as he backed against the wall to try to avoid her. "Stop, Rachel. Just stop. I fucking swear to God." His body shook. His exhausted legs threatened to buckle beneath him. His chest throbbed and vibrated, and so many emotions bombarded him he couldn't keep track of them all. Fucking unreliable is what they were. He thought after a year of beating the bastards into submission they would be trained to stay put, stay buried deep where they belonged. But there he sat, drunk and breaking apart in his sister's living room.

"Please don't push me away," Rachel cried. "Not anymore. Stop pushing everything and everyone away. Face this, Ian. Deal with what happened. So you can move on."

Ian stared at her through tear-filled eyes. He could see the pain and emotion and concern almost falling off her, behind her eyes, in her voice, pulsating through her fingertips and out toward him, but he wasn't ready to give in to his emotions. He couldn't. Pain, pity, fear; shit like those made you *weak*. And he couldn't let himself be weak. Not anymore. He had let himself be weak when he tried to win Sam back and got him nothing but a big fat fucking *No*.

"Leave me the fuck alone, Rachel." She still didn't listen, shaking her head, crying, moving closer and closer to him as he inched farther and farther away. Then her hands were on his, squeezing them, moving up his arms. He cried harder now, so many things he had refused to face clawing their way out.

He tried to fend off his sister's pity and concern. Tried to be strong. Stand tall. But he *was* weak. At least at the moment. Too weak and too tired and he just didn't want to fucking do any of this anymore. He didn't want to cry. He didn't want to try to do good. *Be* good. Fighting for a life that didn't want him to win left him so fucking tired. Tired of searching for happiness he probably didn't even deserve.

He was done.

His legs gave up on him and he slid down the wall to the floor and cried harder than he had ever cried in his life as Rachel held him. He cried because he had lost his parents. He cried because he had lost Sam.

He cried because he had lost himself.

Ian had always been high-strung. But he usually had been able to channel his excess energy and hardheadedness into productive things like getting good grades, making new friends. Hell, his classmates had voted him Most Likely to Succeed in high school, for fuck's sake. He had everything right there in front of him, just waiting for him to reach out and take life as his own. He graduated in the top fifteen of his class. Got a scholarship to college. Met Sam and fell crazy, wholeheartedly in love with him. His life far exceeded anything he could have ever imagined. Then Rachel called one night while he and Sam were at the movies to tell him about his parents and the crash and their deaths and his world incinerated. He no longer cared about good grades or making friends or going to college or, yes, even Sam. Now, a year later, he lay curled up on the floor of his dead parents' house crying in his sister's arms for everything he once had but lost.

Rachel had been right.

He was broken.

Chapter Thirty-Two

Ian had no idea how long he and Rachel stayed on the floor crying their souls out before she helped him upstairs and into bed, but judging how he felt when he woke up, they had sat there for hours. His entire body felt like he had lost a game of chicken against a fucking semi; every inch of him hurt like hell. His back throbbed worse than usual. His head pounded. His legs, already weak from the beating and weeks of intense physical therapy, wobbled like a newborn deer as he walked to the bathroom. And his face. Jesus. Like Brad Pitt after getting the shit beat out of him in *Fight Club*. His eyes were almost swollen shut, dark, puffy circles bigger than before making them appear sunken in like a skull. His cheeks were streaked from his tears, track marks letting the world know, "hey everybody, I'm a big baby who cries all the damn time". God, the fucking crying. He still hated the fact he broke down and gave in to the emotions he had spent so much time and energy fighting off. And to make things worse, he had bared his soul in front of somebody. Which meant he couldn't hide or pretend the crying had never happened.

But he had to admit he did feel better. He didn't know if better was the right word, but there was something that felt different inside him, he could tell. Like when you cram all night and then pass a huge test the next day, and you can let go of all the pressure. Good, better, the word didn't matter, only how he felt like a changed man. He splashed water on his face, trying to wash away some of the ugly and salvage the mess left underneath, and headed downstairs. By the time he poured a cup of much-needed coffee, he had to admit he felt...*good.* Yeah, good summed him up nicely.

"Oh, God, *yes*," Rachel said when she joined him in the kitchen. She moved like a zombie, eyes puffy and half open, arms hanging like a puppet's out in front of her as she reached for some coffee. He slid a cup over to her and she didn't say another word until she had finished assaulting the steaming brew. "I feel so hung over," she said, now sipping the coffee left in her cup.

"You sound like you're dead," Ian added with a smile.

"Have you heard yourself this morning, Sunshine?" She cut her eyes at him. "Or *seen* yourself? Jesus, if I look half as bad as you, I'm going back to bed for about a week."

Ian shoved her and she laughed. "Fuck you, you *wish* you could be this sexy all the time."

"Well obviously you skipped the mirror."

Ian shrugged. "Nothing a long, hot shower won't fix."

"Unless you hook our pipes up to the Fountain of Youth, you're gonna need a hell of a lot more than a shower."

"Wow. Kick a man while he's wallowing in his own self-pity, why don't ya?"

Rachel finished off her coffee and headed to the pot for a refill. "No," she said with a shake of her head. "You *were* wallowing. This is you on your way back up."

"Shit, if this is what climbing the hill feels like, I'll take a hard pass."

Rachel rolled her eyes. "I'm serious, Ian. Last night was—"

"Fucking embarrassing," he interrupted.

"*A good thing*. I would call last night a good thing. A good thing you needed. Hell, I think *I* needed it too."

"You? Miss Always-In-Touch-With-My-Feelings-Twenty-Four-Seven? Get the fuck out."

Rachel punched his upper arm. "Stop being mean." He laughed. "I'm serious, though," she went on. "I needed to go through this with you. I guess I had been avoiding the truth almost as much as you were. But letting go of the pain, the guilt... God, feels *so* good. It *was* good. For both of us."

Ian nodded as he stood up and headed for the sink. He gave his mug a quick rinse and flipped it upside down onto the cheap plastic dish drainer. Unlike his addicted sister, he couldn't stomach more than one cup. "Whatever you say. Let's just never fucking talk about last night again. Sound good?"

Rachel smiled. "I promise nothing." Ian gave her the finger over his shoulder on his way out before heading upstairs to hop in the shower and wash away some of the shame.

*

When he came downstairs close to half an hour later fully dressed even though he had jack shit to do, Rachel had disappeared. She left a note telling him to keep his chin up and take the day for himself and yada yada yada. She could be cheesy as hell sometimes, but Ian smiled and shook his head. "Such a dork," he said with a laugh as he tossed the note in the trash. He grabbed some water from the fridge, scooped up the newspaper off the bar, and headed out to the porch. The temperature felt almost as cold as last night had been, but he welcomed the fresh, clean air. Breathing in the cold made his lungs feel good. Alive. Cleansing. And Ian could use as much cleansing as he could get. With his day wide open, he figured lazing around and enjoying his newfound feelings sounded like a plan. He slid one of the distressed white rocking chairs over so he could prop his feet on the railing and took a seat. Opened the paper. Scanned the articles but not paying much attention to one headline or the other. Until he got to the Announcements page. Right there, at the top, all big and in his face, were Sam and Noah.

Their fucking wedding announcement.

Ian sat up straight in his seat and stared at the picture of the two of them. His first thought: this had to be some sort of milestone, his small, unimportant town having a same-sex wedding announcement in the one and only newspaper. His second: how fucking happy Sam seemed. Ian had seen Sam happy before, but this... This scared the hell out of him.

They were both smiling ear to ear in the cheesy fucking way couples smile in wedding announcement photos. Noah stood behind Sam with his hand on Sam's shoulder, which said a shit ton about their relationship, and Ian couldn't help but laugh a little at the thought. Ian's heart hurt like a bitch seeing Sam touched by somebody else in such a tender way and he wanted a drink so bad the need nearly killed him.

Shit.

He wouldn't go there. Not yet. Not until he saw Sam again. *Sober.* He jumped up, ran back inside to throw on his shoes and coat, and left the house.

He ran almost the entire way to Sam's house, his nerves alive and on edge. Snow had begun to fall, small, thin flakes which somehow managed to stick when they landed even though the air felt too damp. The sun hid behind large gray clouds like a scared child peeking at a stranger through his momma's legs, which only made the frigid temperature feel a dozen degrees colder. But Ian didn't care. He ran through the cold. His breath froze instantly, puffs of clouds smacking him in the face with each huff he took. He ignored the pain shooting up his legs, protesting the assault he constantly put them through, and kept on running. Anxiety consumed him, practically set his skin on fire. What if this didn't work? What if going to Sam and trying to stop him from making a huge mistake blew up in his damn face? What if Sam was still too scared to admit what he wanted and stayed with Noah? Followed through and married the jerk?

"Fuck no." Ian shook the crazy thought from his head. He couldn't think about the possibility. He had to stay focused. He had to trust Sam. Trust he would make the right choice and things would all work out.

His heart thrummed like mad in his ears and his head throbbed by the time he reached the steps leading up to Sam's door. His breathing had moved well beyond labored, his lungs a forest fire in his chest. They were almost screaming at him, his breath coming out in short rapid bursts. He took his time climbing up onto the porch to avoid slipping on the ice coating each wooden step, holding his breath until he had both feet planted on a solid, ice-free surface. Okay, no turning back. Too late to chicken out now, to tuck his tail between his legs and slink home and bury his head in the sand or the bottom of a bottle like he would have in the past. No. No matter how fucking scared he felt, he was more scared to not even try.

He was doing this.

He took a deep breath and knocked. He tensed up when he heard footsteps on the other side like a cornered animal ready to fight to the death. He had already prepared an apology if Noah answered. He wanted to knock the fucking guy out, no doubt, and scoop Sam up and run off with him. But he had heard so much shit about the high road he decided he should see how choosing the less-traveled way felt. So, he would just have to go against his instinct to break the prick's nose and apologize to Noah for interfering.

Turned out he wouldn't have to. Not yet anyway, because when the door opened Sam stood there staring back at him. Ian smiled.

"Hey," he said, his voice shaky, nervous. He wouldn't lie, he was fucking scared to death.

"What are you doing here?" Sam had the door open just enough for his head to poke through.

"I, uh, just wanted to say sorry. Again." Jesus, how many times had he and Sam done this already? "For yesterday. The kiss. I was a dick and—"

"Ian, stop. Please. You don't need to apologize anymore." Sam joined him out on the porch. He wore a chunky sweater with a thick cuff high around his neck, but he still wrapped his arms around himself the second the bitter Chicago winter slammed into him. "Actually, I'm the one who should be apologizing to you. Again."

"What? No, you shouldn't. I'm the problem, Sam. You didn't do anything wrong." Ian wanted to reach out and touch Sam so bad right then. He wanted to pull him close and keep him warm and safe from the cold. He clasped his fidgety hands together instead.

"Noah did," Sam said, his words taking Ian by surprise. What the hell had Noah done? Sam gestured to some chairs and a small table in the middle of the porch and led them over to sit. "I just found out he came to see you. He never should have gone to your house. And he *never* should have punched you. I'm so sorry he did, Ian. He crossed a line."

Ian shook off Sam's words with a shake of his head. "I'm okay," he said. "And please don't apologize for other people, Sam. You had to do enough apologizing when we were together." Sam smiled but the sentiment never reached his eyes and Ian's heart cracked open again. "Besides," he went on, "I would've done the same damn thing."

Sam smiled. "You? You would have killed him." They shared a laugh which tugged on Ian's emotions. "Remember the baseball game we went to in Atlanta? When some guy thought he would steal your parking spot?"

Ian smirked. "Oh yeah, I remember. Fucking jerk got what he deserved."

"You almost got us kicked out before we even got inside," Sam said. "And I don't think he *deserved* the broken nose you probably gave him. Not over a parking spot."

"Okay, he got a little more than he deserved."

"You think?"

"But he was an asshole," Ian protested. "And he treated you like shit. No way I'm ever letting somebody be mean to you." An instant, uncomfortable awkwardness hung in the air. Ian could see they both felt the mounting silence hanging like a rancid odor between them. Jesus, he was fucking this up again.

"I mean it, Sam," Ian went on, trying to break the unwanted tension he'd created. "I'll never let anyone hurt you."

Sam shook his head. Shifted in his seat. "Ian—"

"Don't," Ian interrupted. "Don't say anything. Please. Let me say what I need to say." Sam closed his mouth and just stared at Ian. Ian unclenched the fists he hadn't even realized his hands had created and rested his palms on his thighs. "I just... I wanted you to know something, Sam," he began, his voice catching in his throat. He could feel tears threatening to rise up inside him and he rapid-blinked them back. "I want you to know that no matter what happens, you'll always have me. I will always be here when you need me. When you need anything. I'll always have your back." He swallowed the lump clogging his throat. "Even after you marry Noah, I'll still be here."

Sam's eyes shifted from somber to surprised in seconds. The muscles in his forearms flexed and coiled as he bore down on the armrests of his chair. "How did you know?" he asked, his voice just above a whisper.

Ian wanted to tell him how Noah had happily filled him in, telling him all about the engagement the day he showed up at Ian's door and knocked him into a wall. "Newspaper," he said instead, and Sam nodded in understanding. "The newspaper is why I'm here, to be honest," Ian added.

"What, to congratulate us?" Ian heard the hesitation behind Sam's words. The fear. Like he worried Ian had come there to stop him. Ian knew him better than even he himself realized.

Ian swallowed back his own fear and said, "To beg you not to marry him."

Sam exhaled and shot up out of the chair. "Ian, please stop doing this," he snapped. "I am begging you. You have to stop."

"Don't, Sam," Ian said with a shake of his head. "Don't keep pushing me away. I...I came to say something. Please just let me finish and I'll leave. Okay?" Sam stood there silent, staring down at him. Ian wanted nothing more than to pull him close and kiss him and never fucking stop kissing him until everything wrong turned right and everything bad turned good. When Sam didn't protest further, Ian let out his pent-up breath.

"I'm sorry," he said. "For... God, for every fucking thing. I'm sorry for all the times I've hurt you. For our first argument, when I knew I was wrong and you were right but I kept pushing anyway.

I'm sorry for all the times I know I made you feel unimportant. Or less than. Not good enough. I never ever wanted you to feel like you didn't matter or weren't enough for me. I'm the one who wasn't good enough. Not you. Never you." Ian stood and closed the gap between them as he spoke, never taking his eyes off Sam. And Sam seemed fixated on Ian too, watching him with such intensity he almost scared Ian into silence. He could see he had managed to finally break through Sam's tough, thick exterior, reaching in and reigniting something inside him. Knowing Sam finally heard him only fueled him. Seeing him come alive listening to his words, even if only a little, told Ian had done the right thing.

"And I'm sorry for leaving, Sam," he went on. "I am so fucking sorry for leaving more than anything else." He moved closer. Closer. Sam took a step back, but Ian didn't stop. "Of all the things I'm sorry for, things I regret in my shitty life, walking away from you like I did is by far the biggest regret I have. You didn't deserve to be hurt by my leaving."

"No, I didn't." Sam said, his voice weak, cracking with emotion he clearly tried to hide. Ian stood mere inches from him now. So close he could smell Sam's natural musk. The aroma permeated his senses, set him on fire with want. But he held back. Resisted the overwhelming urge to reach out to Sam. To touch him.

"I'm sorry I couldn't do better by you," Ian said. "I wanted to. God, I fucking wanted to. When my parents died, I knew you were there. I saw you. Felt you. But I was..." Ian's voice caught in his throat as his own emotions gripped him, squeezed his heart until pain leaked out. "I was too far gone to let you in. Let you be there for me. Such a fucking idiot, I know. Realizing just how big an idiot took a long fucking time, and almost killed me, but I understand now. And I could spend the rest of my life trying to make things up to you and I wouldn't even come close to doing enough."

"You don't owe me anything," Sam said, his voice soft and sincere. "Not anymore."

Ian smiled when he noticed Sam wringing his hands. His nervous tick. Watching him warmed Ian's broken heart.

"Yes, I do," he said, finding Sam's eyes again. "I owe you everything, Sam. You are the only reason I'm here. The only reason I'm still alive."

Sam shook his head. "No, don't put this on me, Ian. I don't want to have to try to live up to some impossible version of me you have in your head. It's not fair."

"I didn't mean literally," Ian said. "I just... Thinking of you, has kept me going." Sam looked confused and fear tickled Ian's nerves. He couldn't lose him now. Not when he had gotten so close to breaking through. "What I mean is..." Shit, he couldn't get the words right. He took a deep breath and closed his eyes. Refocused. "I left because I had to. I *had* to. Staying would have—I wouldn't have survived if I had stayed. Yeah, stupid, I know. And I'm a complete fucking prick for leaving without even telling you why or saying good-bye. But... The walls were closing in on me. Fast. Too fast to stop them. When I saw a chance to escape before they crushed me, I jumped. You got hurt in the process, and hurting you fucking kills me."

"I was..." Sam began to cry. Tears flooded his cheeks. Ian had been so focused on getting everything out he wanted to say, so intent on telling Sam everything, he hadn't even noticed Sam's mood. He had hurt the one person he claimed to love above everybody else all over again, just like he swore he wouldn't do. "You *destroyed* me, Ian," Sam said through the tears and the pain. "Your leaving destroyed me." He wiped at the unrelenting deluge pouring out of him.

Ian brushed away his own tears. "God, Sam..." He reached out to touch him, but Sam recoiled so he stopped. He could only stand there and watch as the man he loved fell apart. "I will never forgive myself for hurting you back then," he continued. "Or for hurting you now. I never wanted to hurt you again." His heart crumbled seeing Sam fight the pain he had buried. Pain Ian had caused because he had been too damned selfish to think of somebody other than himself. Seeing Sam hurt made Ian think of his own pain. He had worked so hard to wall up deep inside himself the things hurting him, and he knew just how easily the pain could destroy him if it were ever set free. Like Sam's had destroyed him. Jesus, he didn't want to be the reason Sam became broken like him. He didn't want to be the reason Sam became *anything* like him.

Not anymore.

"I'm leaving," he whispered, the words shocking him as if they had come from someone else, some other pathetic human being admitting defeat. And they were the complete opposite of what he had wanted to say when he read their wedding announcement in the paper. "I'm sorry for this. I never *ever* meant to hurt you. Or for you to get hurt. Please know that, Sam. And know I still love you. I'm still *in love* with you. If you don't remember anything else I said tonight, please remember I love you." Sam stared at him, the blue of his eyes almost glowing behind his tears. Those eyes he loved so damned much gave Ian the strength he needed to say, "And I know I shouldn't ask you this. Or anything, really. I know I'm the last person on earth who should be asking you to do anything for me, but... Please wait for me, Sam."

"Wh—what?" Sam asked.

"I know I've fucked everything up," Ian said. "Fucked *us* up. And I know I'm gonna have to work a lifetime to fix things. To put things back the way they should be." Ian couldn't hold back any longer and took Sam's hand in his own. Sam didn't pull away. "But I *will* fix this," he went on. "I'm gonna fix myself. So I can be the man you want. The man you deserve. I promise you. I just... I need you to wait for me, Sam. Wait for me to fix things. To fix myself. Don't marry him. Don't love him. Love me. Love us. Wait for *us*."

The world around them disappeared as Ian held all the air in his lungs until they were screaming at him to breathe. Only he and Sam existed in this moment. Nothing else mattered. Nothing at all. Ian had finally done what he had railed against the past year. He had almost destroyed himself trying to avoid this. Had fought tooth and nail and drank and smoked and swallowed every shot and joint and drug he could find to resist the urge clawing at him. But in the end, he lost the battle. He gave in. And though he had never ever wanted to, he gave in and bared his soul. The fucking ugliest parts of himself were out there now, in the open for all to see and laugh and gawk at like a carnival sideshow freak. Now, whatever would or wouldn't happen sat in Sam's hands.

"Ian," Sam said, his words soft and broken and full of something Ian didn't want to hear. His stomach dropped.

God, he was going to say no.

After Ian had poured his heart, bloody and beaten down, out to him, Sam would just finish him off by saying no. He would just keep ignoring his true feelings and marry a man he didn't love. And Ian would lose him all over again. Forever.

"Don't." Ian said, shaking his head. He let Sam's hand fall away, his fingertips lingering as long as possible so he could savor every millimeter of Sam's skin in case he never got to feel his warmth again. "Please don't say anything. Not yet. Just promise me you'll think about everything I said." He brought a hand up and rested his palm against Sam's chest. Sam's heart beat fast like a hummingbird's, an exuberant, electric rhythm which somehow calmed Ian down. He felt electrified, like a live wire, and Ian could only hope Sam felt even a fraction of the same way he did.

"I will," Sam answered. Ian smiled because he knew even though his words were shaky and sounded unsure, Sam wouldn't lie. Without hesitation he leaned in and stole a kiss, then left with something he hadn't had in a long time.

Hope.

Chapter Thirty-Three

Ian had become a complete fucking wreck by the time he made his way home. His eyes were thick as marshmallows from all the crying. His nose ran like a five-year-old's. His head was stuck in a wood splitter. His legs and back felt like he had run home from the other side of the fucking country. He had spent the walk from Sam's flip-flopping back and forth on whether Sam would wait for him like he had asked him to or run from the truth and marry Noah. The not knowing drove him fucking insane.

He had to stop dwelling on what may or may not happen. As hard as he knew relinquishing control would be, he had to. He had to let go to keep his sanity. He needed to focus instead on the promise he had made to Sam, the promise he would work to fix things. Fix himself.

The mere thought scared the shit out of him. Made him want to get so fucking drunk and high he would forget his own name. But he knew he had to do something. He couldn't keep turning to alcohol or drugs every time he got scared or freaked the fuck out. Not if he ever wanted Sam back. Sam didn't deserve such a life.

And if Ian were being honest with himself, he didn't deserve one either. He had beaten himself down enough. Blamed himself for shit he had no control over. Now he needed to grow a backbone and stand up again. Stand up for himself.

*

"You ready?" Rachel brought the last suitcase downstairs and dropped the ugly brown lump full of Ian's clothes by the front door.

"As ready as I'm gonna be, I guess." Ian helped carry the luggage out to the car and loaded each piece into the trunk before moving around to the passenger door. He took a second to turn back toward Rachel's house. *His* house.

"Man, I did *not* wanna come back here," he said, more to himself than anyone. "I mean, I *really* didn't wanna come back here."

"Okay, okay," Rachel said, adjusting the suitcases he had tossed in the trunk so the lid would close.

Ian smiled. "Now, though, I think I'm gonna miss this house. Sounds crazy right?"

"You're only gonna be gone three months, Ian," Rachel said, slamming the trunk shut and rounding the car to the driver's side. "You'll be home in no time, and then you'll have the rest of your life to hate living here."

Ian opened the passenger door. "A few months can feel like a thousand sometimes." That had for sure been the case with Sam. Only two weeks had gone by since Ian had bared his soul and Sam hadn't reached out once, one way or the other. He hadn't told Ian if he stood a chance or lay dead in the water.

"Try to look at this like a vacation," Rachel said. Her words pulled Ian's thoughts away from Sam and the what-ifs.

"Oh yeah," he said with thick sarcasm. "I've always wanted to spend ninety days talking about how fucking screwed up I am while sitting around with a bunch of strangers who'll probably end up being more fucked up than me. Sounds like a dream."

Rachel smiled and they both got in the car. "Well," she said as they pulled away from the curb, "how about a sort of reset, then? You can relax and clear your head and get rid of all the stuff you stay so worked up over."

Ian shrugged. "Yeah, sounds good." He stared out the window as the town he had hated most of his life growing up passed them by, growing smaller and smaller as they got farther and farther away. He would miss Any Town, USA too, which surprised the hell out of him.

"You scared?" Rachel asked.

"Fucking terrified." A battle raged inside him, trying to keep his fear in check while at the same time opening himself up to deal with what scared him. Ian had been raging war since his parents died. And he fucking hated the fight.

"Of what?"

He kept his eyes locked on the crazy blur of trees and grass flowing past his window as Rachel drove. They were well out of town now, dense forest the only thing lining the highway on both sides. He didn't know how to answer her question. What the hell *was* he scared of? The easiest answer? Everything. Scared of failing like he always did whenever he tried to right a wrong. Scared of how fucked up life would be if he never got to have a drink again. And fucking *terrified* of the type of person he would be once he got sober. And he couldn't forget the chance he might be alone the rest of his life if Sam didn't come back to him.

How the hell could he sum up his fear?

"Myself," he said. "I'm scared of myself. Of whether or not I can do this."

"Of course you can," Rachel said with confidence Ian wouldn't swear on a bible was real. "You are the strongest person I know, Ian." He scoffed. "I'm serious. You brought yourself out of some pretty heavy shit to get to this point."

"Yeah, shit I did to myself."

"Exactly. Your problems aren't because of something you can't control. Something you can't fix. They're because of *you*. Which means you can change them. You can change yourself. So you don't make the same mistakes again." Rachel reached over and gave his arm a firm but tender squeeze. "You got this, little brother. Trust me."

Ian tried to trust what Rachel said. He wanted to believe he had this. Wanted to believe he could walk through the pain he had ignored all this time and come out new and whole on the other side. He swallowed back his fear and put his hand over hers. "I love you, you dork."

"Back at ya, doofus."

They spent the next hour or so in relative silence, a few comments about traffic and the weather and Rachel saying how empty the house would feel with him gone until Ian asked, "Will you do me a favor while I'm gone?"

"Of course," Rachel answered.

He took a deep breath, fighting back tears. He couldn't cry. He wouldn't. Not today. "Keep an eye on him for me? Make sure he's okay?"

Rachel gave him a knowing look and smiled. "Of course."

Ian nodded and stared out the window again. Knowing Rachel would watch out for Sam, make sure he stayed safe and more importantly, happy, set him at ease. He could go knowing the one person in the world who mattered most to him would have someone watching his back while Ian couldn't. For the first time in a long time,

Ian felt peaceful. Almost happy. Sure, he fucking hated not being with Sam. But he couldn't be a thousand percent sure now having Sam in his life topped his list of things most important to him. He still felt crazy in love with the man, no denying that ever, but... Maybe the time had come for him to try to fix himself. To put himself first. Start appreciating, for better or worse, his life belonged to him again and not whatever bottle or pill he could find.

The mere idea of having so much power and control over his future scared the shit out of him. Life since his parents died—and even before then, if he told the truth—had been a never-ending war over whether or not every decision he had made or would make would be the one to send him spiraling back to rock bottom. He had a long way to go before he trusted himself to choose the right path going forward.

The one thing he had zero doubt about, though, was telling Sam how he felt. Even if pouring his heart out had been the right thing to do, regardless of what Sam decided, he was still terrified. And in the end, above all else, he just wanted Sam to be happy.

And he wanted happiness for himself now too.

*

"Take care of yourself in there, okay?" Rachel said once they got to where they were going and climbed out of the car. She pulled him into a hug and squeezed him tighter and held him longer than she ever had, and Ian couldn't have been happier. He hugged her back, searing into his memory how great he felt having a sister who never let him down.

"I will," he said. "And thanks."

She pulled back and stared up at him. "For what?"

"For everything," he said. "For kicking my ass for being an idiot. Making sure I didn't fuck things up so bad they can't be fixed." He brushed a tear from her cheek. "You've been everything to me, Rach. Mom. Dad. Sister. Hell, my warden sometimes." She punched his arm and they both laughed. "My best friend," he added. "You're my best friend. Better than most people would have been through all my shit. I...I love you, sis."

Rachel cried too hard to speak, so she just kept hugging him. And Ian hugged her just as hard. He held out as long as he could, relishing the love he and his sister had found again. He cherished their relationship, the only one in his life he could count on, no matter how much he screwed up. Even though he would miss Sam with everything he had, he thought he just might miss Rachel even more.

"I gotta go," he said, sliding his arms behind him and unclasping her hands. "I don't think they would like me showing up late on my first day of rehab."

"Screw them," she said, holding tight to his waist even though he had pulled away. She finally gave up and dropped her arms. "Stay here with me. I'll be your rehab."

Ian brought his hands to her cheeks. Held her. Wiped her tears. "You already are," he said, then walked inside.

Epilogue

"I don't know about this, Rach." Nerves tickled his skin like mosquitos as he fished his suitcases out of the trunk of her car. Like an elephant had passed out on his fucking chest. Crushing weight pushed in on his lungs. He fought to catch his breath.

"Relax." Rachel rubbed his back. "I only invited a *very* small group, I swear. Some nurses from the hospital, your friend Josh. You'll be fine. Promise." She took the bag Ian had a death grip on and hooked the strap over her shoulder. She raised the handle on his larger suitcase and rolled the piece of luggage behind her as she gave her brother a nudge toward the house. He started fidgeting as he walked, twisting and pulling on his hands like they were somebody else's and he would die if he didn't rip them from his body. He kept his eyes on them. Stared at them.

Thought of Sam.

"Fuck." He stopped walking and just stood there in the driveway in the freezing cold, staring down at his hands as tears filled his eyes.

"What?" Rachel asked. "What's wrong?"

He shook his head. "Nothing. I just... Sam wrings his hands when he's nervous. Or upset. Or pretty much all the time. At least he did. I don't know if he does anymore." He didn't know what Sam did anymore.

"Ian..."

He faked a smile. "I'm fine. Really." He let go of his hands and took a deep breath. Let the crisp winter air and beginnings of a snowfall fill his lungs. Clear his head. He had been gone just over three months, even though he felt in some ways like no more than a day had passed. "I know I gotta move on to be healthy and happy and shit. I get it. I just... I still miss him, you know? Still love him. That's all. I swear I'm not gonna wig out or get wasted or anything." He held up three fingers. "Scout's honor."

"You were never a scout," she said with a smirk. "And I wasn't even thinking such a thing, thank you very much. I just hate seeing you upset."

"Really? I figured you'd be used to me falling apart by now." He nudged her with his elbow and smiled. "I promise I'm okay. Or, I will be. I can do this, I know I can now." He tried to convince Rachel just as much as himself.

Would he be okay? Would he really? He didn't know. Not for sure. Not yet, anyway. The endless therapy he had gotten in rehab said he would—"That which doesn't kill us makes us stronger"—but he had no way of knowing for sure. Not until he bit the bullet and took the first step. One day at a time, just like the program said. Which fucking sucked, because now more than ever he wanted to blink and be in the future. A future where he had moved past all of his issues, past Sam, past the pain. He desperately wanted to be happy.

He closed his eyes. Tried to wish such a life into existence.

"I know you can." Rachel's voice brought him back. Back to the present, where he was still alone and Sam had married someone else.

Fuck. *Sam's married.*

Ian had been so focused on fixing himself, on getting better and figuring out what doing so actually meant, he had almost forgotten Sam and Noah were married now. They had stood in front of their friends and family and exchanged vows and kissed and fucked like crazy on their honeymoon while Ian sat in rehab crying about how much he wanted to be the guy Sam did all those things with. He thanked God he had missed their wedding. Glad he had been locked away where he couldn't ruin their big day. Because God knows he would have. He would have tried everything to stop Sam from giving his heart to someone else. Promising to love and honor and cherish another man until death.

The elephant on his chest got comfortable, settling in for the long haul.

"You sure you're okay?" Rachel asked, watching him. "If you're seriously freaking out about the party"—she gestured to the house, where who knew how many people were waiting to see him, welcome him home like he'd been away at summer camp or college—"I can make everybody leave. Just say the word."

He wanted to—damn, he wanted to—but he couldn't. If he wasn't able to face his first test, he might as well turn around and go back to rehab and check himself in for the rest of his fucking life.

"No, I'm fine," he said. "Really. I'm kind of excited to see everybody." He had no fucking clue who Rachel had invited. They didn't have extended family as far as he knew, and the only people in his life he called a friend were Stacey and Josh, but he knew he had to stop whining and face life. So, he fought the urge to turn and run. He didn't want to be the kind of guy who is scared to face things anymore. He fucking *hated* that guy. He wanted to stand up and face the shit he didn't like. Deal with his issues, the problems life threw in his face. Like unwanted welcome-home parties. He grabbed Rachel's hand and squeeze her fingers in his a little too hard. "Let's do this."

*

Ian slipped out of the party and onto the front porch, desperate for some fresh air and time alone. Since he had stepped foot through the door about an hour ago, he had been bombarded by well-wishers and congratulatory smiles and pats on the back. Most of the people there were from Rachel's work, so he didn't *know them* know them, but there were a few faces he recognized from the weeks he spent in the hospital. Seeing Elaine again lifted his spirits. And Josh was just as in-your-face insane as always, which made Ian laugh and calmed his jittery nerves a bit. Stacey hadn't been able to get away from Final Draft, but Rachel said she sent her love, which just sounded weird coming from Stacey. At least his sister hadn't lied; she kept the crowd to just under fifteen. Fourteen too many for him.

He had wanted to just come home and relax on his first day back. Hang with his sister. Get acclimated to being on his own again, out of the controlled environment of rehab where his problems didn't matter because they couldn't hurt you in there. He sure as hell didn't want to face people talking about how proud they were of him. Compliments made him uncomfortable because he didn't feel proud by any means. He felt like a fucking failure. Twenty-five and a stint in rehab under his belt. No job, no home, no one to hold when things got hard. All the doctors and therapists and sharing his feelings and shit had taught him how feeling down and hating yourself were a normal part of the process, but knowing sure as hell didn't make things easier to face.

He rested his arms on the porch railing and stared out at the neighborhood. Streetlamps pocked the quiet darkness, lighting the way for anybody dumb enough to take a walk in the middle of nowhere during a Chicago winter. Snow began to fall heavier now, a thin blanket coating everything Ian could see. He shivered against the cold as he eyed the houses lining the street, their cookie-cutter styles monotonous and somewhat soothing. After the year he'd had, he welcomed the monotony. He had begun to crave the boring and predictable. Crazy and *un*predictable shit need not apply.

Ian exhaled and stretched, letting the anxiety from the party and being back home fall away. He could do this. He would survive. He didn't know how just yet, but he knew he would. He had come too damn far not to.

"That bad, huh?"

He jumped.

The voice. *His* voice.

Ian's eyes were drawn to the sound. Saw him. Smiled. Bigger than he had since the day they had first met.

He managed to reign his excitement in a bit. "Worse," he joked as he headed for the steps leading down to the yard.

"Stay there. I'll come up." Ian stopped. Watched Sam make his way through the snow and up the icy walkway. Up the steps. Before he could take a breath Sam stood in front of him, as if he had always been there. Like the past had never happened.

"Hi," Ian said, the words struggling to come out. He kept smiling. He hoped he never stopped.

"Hey, you." Sam smiled back, and all the fear and worry and doubt Ian had about what life would be like after rehab began to dissipate. Sam was there. Right there in front of him, flesh and bone and the beautiful smile he would never get tired of seeing. Ian didn't care why Sam had come. He knew now everything would be okay.

"You're not wearing your contacts." He gestured to Sam's eyes. He had been fixated on them from the second Sam stepped onto the porch.

Sam adjusted his black-rimmed glasses. "Oh. Yeah." He flashed a crooked little smile, making Ian melt. His heart beat so hard and fast in his chest; he thought it would explode. His pulse lead the way in a fucking marathon. His palms were sweaty as shit. Jesus, what Sam did to him with only a smile...

Doubt snuck up on him. Blindsided him. He wanted to ignore the feeling but knew he couldn't. His doubt had been right before. He couldn't let himself be swept up by Sam again. He had to stop. As much as he didn't want to, he had to stop.

"What're you doing here?" he asked, breaking eye contact and glancing out at the falling snow. The white flakes bouncing and tumbling through the air were beautiful against the night sky, lit up by tiny pops of light from streetlamps skirting the sidewalk at the foot of the yard. The scenery helped distract Ian from the tall slab of perfect standing on his porch. He looked back at Sam. Then at the door behind him. The door he should have been walking through instead of standing there falling helplessly off a cliff.

"Oh. Uh, I thought you knew I was coming? Rachel said—"

"Rachel knew you'd be here?"

"She's the one who invited me," Sam answered. "And welcome home, by the way."

Ian rolled his eyes and turned and walked down the porch. "Please, not you too."

Sam followed him. "What? What did I say?"

"I wasn't off fighting for our country or saving lives in some third-world shithole. I was in rehab for fuck's sake. *Rehab.* I wish everybody would—I shouldn't be welcomed back like some kind of fucking hero." He cut his eyes at Sam. "And you shouldn't be here." His throat bled from the words. "Go home, Sam. Go home to your husband."

Sam stared at him for a few seconds before a smile spread across his face. Which threw Ian off big time.

"I'm not married," Sam said, moving closer to him.

His words took Ian aback. He had to actually *step* back to keep from falling over. "Wait. What? I... I saw the announcement before I left. Didn't you have a wedding, like, two weeks ago? I don't—"

Sam shook his head. "The wedding *would have been* two weeks ago. But I didn't marry Noah."

Ian had jumped onto a merry-go-round again. The same merry-go-round he had visited time and time again for the past two years. And like always, revolutions were at top speed right out of the gate, spinning and spinning and spinning, nowhere to jump off, the world on the outside a blur of upside-down images. Everything he thought he knew, everything he had believed to be the truth shattered in his mind, fractured and splintered, leaving him unsure of even himself.

Sam stood there, right there in front of him. He came because he didn't get married. Because he didn't condemn himself to a life he never wanted. Just like Ian had done back in rehab when he had accepted he and Sam were no longer he and Sam. Realizing what was happening right then almost became too much for Ian's fragile mind to take.

"I don't understand," he said, locking eyes with Sam again. "You didn't get married?" Sam shook his head again. Smiled again. "Why not?"

"Because," Sam began, closing the distance between them. He took Ian's hand in his and Ian's gaze dropped. He had to see for himself to believe what his fingers felt. To believe he hadn't imagined this moment. There were Sam's fingers, laced in his. Gripping his. Together. One. *Them.* "Somebody asked me to wait for him. So, I did."

Ian's entire world exploded the second Sam leaned in and kissed him. Everything he had been through, had put himself through—none of the shit he had endured mattered anymore. The pain. The loss. The fucking relentless heartache. They were forever a part of him, part of what made him, but they no longer defined him or dictated his choices in life. They no longer meant he couldn't be happy or didn't *deserve* to be happy.

Because Sam had shown up for him. Sam loved him. Even after everything he had done to him, to them, Sam still loved him. Wanted him. Waited for him.

As Ian stood on the porch in the middle of the night, kissing the man he loved beneath the falling snow, he never wanted the merry-go-round to stop spinning.

Acknowledgements

As always, a huge thank you to NineStar Press for taking a chance on this story so I can share it with you all.

A great big hug and thank you to my amazingly patient and understanding editor, Stacey Jo, for having the ability to put up with me yet again—you rock!

To the readers who take a chance on an unknown and give this book a read—you guys never cease to amaze.

And for anyone going through substance abuse recovery, thank you for never giving up on yourself.

About the Author

My love of writing began when I bought my very first book when I was barely a tween. It was adult and long and much too mature for my young mind, but it forever changed me and made me fall in love with reading. I love getting lost in the pages of a novel over almost everything else (except maybe TV—that's my jam!), and writing is yet another wonderful escape that hooked me from the start.

I live in a very small, very hot, and humid city in the south, where I long for colder days and am envious of those who see snow every year.

I hope you enjoy reading *Finding Fisher* as much as I enjoyed writing it!

Email: authormjjames@gmail.com

Twitter: @AuthorMJ_James

Website: www.mjjamesauthor.blogspot.com

Other NineStar books by this author

Out of the Ashes

Also Available from NineStar Press

Connect with NineStar Press

www.ninestarpress.com

www.facebook.com/ninestarpress

www.facebook.com/groups/NineStarNiche

www.twitter.com/ninestarpress

www.tumblr.com/blog/ninestarpress